ALEXANDER McCALL SMITH is one of the world's most prolific and most popular authors. For many years he was a professor of Medical Law, then, after the publication of ighly successful No 1 Ladies' Detective Agency series, devoted his time to the writing of fiction. He has seen various series translated into forty-six languages and ome bestsellers throughout the world. These include 44 Scotland Street novels, the Isabel Dalhousie books, well as the Von Igelfeld and Corduroy Mansions series. e lives in Edinburgh.

ALEXANDER McCALL SMITH

FATTY O'LEARY'S DINNER PARTY

Polygon

First published in 2014. This edition published in paperback in Great Britain in 2015 by Polygon, an imprint of Birlinn Ltd
West Newington House
10 Newington Road
Edinburgh EH9 1QS

www.polygonbooks.co.uk

9 8 7 6 5 4 3 2 1

ISBN: 978 1 84697 323 9

British Library Cataloguing-in-Publication Data. A catalogue record for this book is available on request from the British Library.

Typeset by Studio Monachino
Printed and bound by Clays Ltd, St Ives plc

This book is for Hugh Andrew, at last

STARTER

A Tight Squeeze

I

Cornelius Patrick O'Leary had been known as Fatty O'Leary from the time he was twelve, which was in the early 1950s. People were less sensitive then to the feelings of people around them, and many of the nicknames they gave to others were thoughtlessly unkind. Yet in those more robust, not to say careless days, those to whom disparaging nicknames were given sometimes appeared to accept the situation. Or so it seemed on the surface: people suffered in silence then, enduring things that today people simply would not bear, while all the time they smarted under the casual cruelty of a derogatory nickname. Cornelius O'Leary, though, was not like this: he never objected to being called Fatty, and even signed himself as such.

He was a good man, and a kind one. If those who first called him Fatty – those childhood friends, the boys in the boy scouts, the slightly simple man who served sodas in the drug store who delighted in inventing a nickname for every customer – had done so with the intent to belittle or provoke him, then he forgave them; forgiveness came easily to Fatty – it was easier, he thought, to like people than to dislike them, however they behaved towards you.

Dislike required energy and a good memory for slights; geniality was so much less demanding, and at the end of the day felt better too.

He was indifferent to the embarrassed surprise that people sometimes showed when he used the name of himself. "It's simpler than signing Cornelius," he said with a disarming smile. "Two syllables rather than four. It saves time." And then he added, "And I could do to lose a bit round the middle, I suppose – but who couldn't?"

Fatty lived in Fayetteville, Arkansas, a pleasant college town on the edge of the Ozarks. He was the son of a comfortably-off local businessman who owned a small furniture factory, a warehouse, a motel, and a bar that was popular with students from the university. Those were the profitable parts of the family business, but not the interesting bit. That was an antique store that Fatty ran personally, leaving the other concerns in the hands of a manager. Fatty knew a great deal about antique furniture; he had a good eye for it and had even written the occasional article in a furniture magazine published in Boston. He was particularly proud of those articles, which were framed and hung in prominent places round the house.

Fatty's wife was called Betty; she was the former Miss Elizabeth Shaugnessy, of Mobile, Alabama. They had met when they were both at the University of Notre Dame. Betty had fallen in love with Fatty the first time she saw him – and he with her. They were ideally suited, and while most married couples cannot say with complete honesty that they had never fought with one another over anything, Fatty and Betty could do just that.

Fatty's two closest old friends in Fayetteville were Tubby O'Rourke and Porky Flanagan. Tubby was an accountant with an interest in model railways; Porky was a dentist who ran a dental practice set up by his father and his uncle. He did not really enjoy dentistry and had complained to Fatty on more than one occasion that it was his uncle, in particular, who had leant on him to go to dental school.

"All he thinks about is teeth, Fatty. Mention a name and he says, *I know that guy's teeth*. He went to Washington once and came back and complained that there were no statues of dentists."

"He's got a point," said Fatty. "Dentists deserve a few statues. Maybe a few statues to dentists who fell in foreign wars."

Tubby looked thoughtful. "They probably weren't right up there on the front line," he said. "They were fixing teeth back in the field hospitals."

"Yes," said Fatty. "Maybe they were. But we still need dentists."

"We sure do," said Tubby. "Thank God for dentists."

"Okay," said Porky. "We need dentists, but not everyone has to be a dentist, right?"

The three friends used to meet every other week to play poker. Fatty had also taught them Mah Jong, and they occasionally played that, although Tubby did not enjoy it as much as poker, which he almost always won. This was, in fact, a potential source of tension, as Tubby won so often that Porky began to suspect him of cheating. Fortunately he never made a direct accusation to this effect, as Tubby would never have done anything dishonest.

Betty thought Tubby the most handsome man she had ever met. She said that if Tubby had gone to Hollywood, he would almost certainly have been snapped up by the movie people. She once told Tubby this, at a party, and he laughed and said, "You've had too much to drink, Betty. I'd never have got far in the movies: those guys in the movies carry a bit less weight than I do."

Joan O'Rourke, Tubby's wife, said, "Tubby can't act, anyway."

2

THIS IS THE STORY OF the events that took place round Fatty's fortieth birthday in the summer of 1979 when Fatty paid his first visit to Ireland. This trip was Betty's birthday present to her husband, who had long talked about an Irish holiday but who had never seemed to find the time to organise one. Like Betty, Fatty considered himself every bit as Irish as he was American. His credentials for this identity were impeccable: not only was there his name, which was quintessentially Irish, but he could also point to the exact identity of the Irish forebear who had decided that enough was enough. This was his grandfather, also called Cornelius Patrick O'Leary – or Corny P. O'Leary, as he became known – who had emigrated from an obscure corner of County Tipperary to establish the family home in Fayetteville four years before the outbreak of the First World War. Arkansas, with its abundant supplies of timber, was an ideal place for the furniture factory that Corny set up. He had gone to America to get away from everything that he regarded as being wrong with Ireland – persistent rain, congenitally arrogant Anglo-Irish gentry, and a legion of squabbling relatives. Freed of Ireland, he became enthusiastically more Irish than ever before, and set to the establishing of a modest dynasty of O'Learys, centred upon the rambling double-storey house, Tipperary View, that he built in the centre of Fayetteville. It was not at all clear why he should have called the house this. It never had much of a view, and certainly not one of Tipperary, from which it was separated by three thousand miles of ocean and a considerable slice of the American continent; but, as Fatty once remarked to Betty, we see what we want to see in this life, and it was undoubtedly true that if his grandfather had dreamed of seeing anything, it would have been those soft and distant Irish hills.

As Fatty's birthday approached, a visit to Ireland had not been the first possibility Betty explored. She had looked into the feasibility of a week or two in Honolulu, but had decided that Fatty would probably dislike this. Neither of them particularly took to crowds and busy hotels, and she was sure that they would find both of these in Hawaii. Besides, she knew that a trip to Ireland would enable Fatty to seek out the ancestral farm from which the original Cornelius O'Leary had set forth on the fateful day in July, 1910. It was possible that there were still O'Learys there, and to locate some distant relatives would be a bonus. Fatty was proud of the O'Leary family, and would be delighted to make contact with any Irish cousins who might still be lurking in Tipperary. Betty was more cautious: she wondered what sort of unenterprising people would choose to remain in Ireland when they could easily have left the country, even if only to take the ferry to Liverpool. Well, they would soon find out, and if the Irish relatives proved to be at all … at all embarrassing they could be left right there. If, on the other hand, they were promising, they might be persuaded to emigrate, as Betty assumed that all sensible Irish people had either already emigrated to America or were at least actively contemplating doing so. Indeed, it was quite surprising that anybody remained there at all, other than those few needed to act as curators.

Fatty was enthusiastic when he heard that Betty had booked the flights. They were to fly to Dallas and from there they would continue their journey to Shannon. There they could hire a car and drive the short distance to Tipperary.

"How do you picture Ireland, Fatty?" Betty asked dreamily. "Do you have a clear image of it?"

"I certainly do," replied Fatty. "A lush green landscape, dotted with tiny white-washed cottages. And a patchwork of fields."

"And rain?" prompted Betty.

"Oh yes," said Fatty. "Lots of rain."

"Marvellous!" said Betty. "Except perhaps for the rain."

"Gentle rain," went on Fatty, "barely noticeable, Irish rain – quite different from the rain we get out here. A little bit like whiskey, I think. Very weak, but still with the taste of the barley on it."

Betty laughed.

Fatty shook his head fondly. "Oh, Betty," he said, "you're a genius to have thought of all this!"

They had only three weeks to wait. Then, on the morning of their departure, they closed up the house and were driven to the airport by Porky Flanagan. There they caught their plane to Dallas and were eventually herded through to the waiting room for the departure of their flight to Shannon. When he saw the name Shannon on the departure board, Fatty grabbed Betty's arm in excitement.

"I feel we're really on our way now," he said. "Shannon! That's Ireland, Betty! That's Ireland!"

Betty planted a kiss on his cheek. "You've worked hard for this,' she said. "Forty years of hard work."

"Well hardly," said Fatty. "I didn't start working the day I was born. Nobody does. Twenty years perhaps. Seventeen if you don't count college."

"Well that's still a lot of work," said Betty.

Fatty smiled. Betty was quite right: he did deserve a bit of leisure. He had been successful. Indeed, if he wanted to stop working even at forty, he could do so and live very comfortably for the rest of his days. Perhaps a condominium in Florida and a fishing boat for him and … and something or other, a refrigerator perhaps, for Betty. But could he fish? He had never fished before, and he had never played golf. All he knew about, when one came to think about it, was antique tables and the like; if he wanted to busy himself in retirement, then he would have to try to broaden his interests. Betty would be able to amuse herself by putting things in the refrigerator and then taking them out. He wouldn't even have that.

Of course forty was far too early to be thinking about retirement. Some people started a second career at that stage, or even married again and began a family. Fatty could not imagine himself doing that. He and Betty had not had children, but that was just the way things worked out and they had been perfectly happy by themselves. He could not imagine himself ever marrying anybody other than Betty. We've grown forty together, he mused, wondering whether that could ever be made into a song: *We've grown forty together/ We've put on a bit of weight/ We've grown forty together/ But, darling, it's never too late.*

Never too late for what? Fatty was uncertain. The lines certainly had the makings of a popular song, and perhaps one day he would show it to Tubby O'Rourke, who composed songs in his spare time. Tubby had never met with any success with his compositions, but perhaps they could make a team, rather like Rodgers and Hammerstein, or Gilbert and Sullivan. Leary and Rourke sounded quite professional. The new musical by Leary and Rourke: *Forty Years On*. Or perhaps they could have a clever title such as *Forty Years O' O'Leary and O'Rourke*. Possibly, but one should not try to be too clever, he thought.

Fatty looked at his watch. The plane was due to leave at ten p.m. and it was now nine forty-five. If they did not start boarding the passengers soon, he imagined that there would be no possibility of taking off anywhere near the flight's allotted time. But did it mater? They were on holiday and they were going to Ireland, and Ireland was the sort of place, he suspected, that didn't mind when you arrived. You could be a year or two late and they would still welcome you. *Yes, we expected you last year, but the important thing is that you're here, to be sure ...* As he was considering this, the public address system crackled into life.

The airline much regretted it, they were told, but the plane was overbooked. Fortunately it was only overbooked by one passenger, and they were therefore asking for a volunteer to offer to stay behind until tomorrow evening's flight, in return for a cash reward. The passengers sat stony-faced. Nobody stirred.

"Now, ladies and gentlemen," said a disembodied voice. "We must again ask for one passenger to offer to stay behind. An aircraft has a finite number of seats and we cannot take off with somebody standing." The announcer laughed nervously. "So we need one passenger to step forward."

Fatty looked at his shoes. He was certainly not going to volunteer. They had arranged reservations at the other end and, besides, he was now forty. Younger people could give up their seats more easily than middle-aged people – everybody would recognise the justice of that.

There was a knot of discussion at the desk. One of the passengers had approached and was talking to an official.

"Look," said Fatty to Betty. "The volunteer. How good of him. Now we can get on our way."

But the volunteer had now half-turned round and was pointing in Fatty's direction. He said something to the official, who nodded and started to make his way over to Fatty.

"Excuse me, sir," the official said. "It has been suggested to us that you might care to volunteer."

"Good idea!" muttered somebody from a seat behind, to be greeted with a glare from Betty.

"Me?" said Fatty indignantly. "Why me?"

The airline official looked slightly embarrassed. "Well, sir, it appears that you are the ... the largest of the passengers and that most weight would be saved if you were to stay behind. The aircraft really is very full and is up against the weight limit for our fuel load. Almost over it, in fact. If you stayed we would probably be all right. You wouldn't want to be responsible for the aircraft not making it off the runway, would you?"

Fatty's eyes opened wide with outrage. He glanced sideways at Betty, now glaring at the official with an anger matching that of her husband.

"How dare you suggest such a thing!" Fatty exploded. "How dare you pick on me like this!"

The official held up his hands. "I'm sorry, sir," he said. "I don't mean to give offence. I was merely being practical."

"So it's practical to insult your passengers, is it?" blurted out Betty. "Is that the way you treat all stout people, may I ask?"

The official backed away. "I'm terribly sorry," he said.

"Let's leave it. I had no idea you people would be so hyper-sensitive about being so …"

He glanced behind him. One of his colleagues was signalling from the desk.

"Ah," he said. "They've sorted it out. Somebody else has taken up the offer. Please excuse me."

Fatty settled back in his seat.

"I can't recall when I was last so insulted," he muttered to Betty. "I'm going to write to the airline about this."

"You have every right to do just that," agreed Betty, reaching across to touch Fatty on his still-offended arm. "Still, let's not allow it to spoil our holiday. Things will be different in Ireland."

3

BECAUSE OF THE FULLNESS OF the flight and the vagaries of the seat allocation system, Fatty and Betty were separated from one another. Fatty was placed in the front row of the economy cabin, while Betty was seated ten rows behind him, lost in the sea of faces that a large aircraft so quickly becomes. Fatty craned his neck to get a glimpse of his wife, and she waved cheerfully to him before they both settled. Then the procedures of departure began, and they were soon heading north-east, climbing up over Texas, on the very reverse bearing to that pursued by Corny P. O'Leary those many years ago.

Fatty felt uncomfortable. The seats in the economy class of passenger jets are designed for the average frame, and often badly-designed at that. Fatty was far from average, tending, in his words, to the generously proportioned. Although he just managed to squeeze between the armrests of the middle seat in which he was placed, the passengers on either side of him found that their own space was substantially encroached upon by various parts of Fatty. His elbows, which were stout in the extreme, were touching the sides of each neighbour, digging into their chests. His legs, which again were well-covered, were pressed hard against the thighs of each, and every time that Fatty breathed in, the other passengers felt a great pressure against their own chests, requiring them to exhale as he inspired, and vice versa.

It was clearly going to be an impossible trip, and it was not long before the two affected passengers were exchanging surreptitious glances.

"Going to Ireland?" Fatty addressed the man on his right cheerfully.

"Well, that's where this plane's going ..." began his travelling companion, but then Fatty breathed in and the rest of his sentence was cut short.

"And you?" asked Fatty conversationally, turning to the woman on his left. "Have you been to Ireland before?"

She tried to speak, but failed, being virtually winded. She looked imploringly at the man beyond Fatty who nodded in sympathy and reached for the call button to summon help. When the cabin attendant arrived, Fatty's neighbour rose from his seat, pushing hard on Fatty's elbow to allow him to do so, and engaged in an earnest, whispered conversation with the attendant.

The attendant appreciated the situation and sought to reassure the distressed passenger. Making her way forward, she found the purser, who discreetly peered at the source of the problem.

"The only free seat is up in First Class," the purser said. "We were keeping places for a couple of VIPs who called off at the last moment. Move him up there. That'll give the others some room."

Fatty was delighted. It was a small First Class cabin, with only ten seats, each of which occupied the space of at least two economy seats. In the middle of the cabin was a large, fixed table on which a flower arrangement was secured, along with a row of bottles of wine. Fatty, who had a good eye for these matters, could tell at a glance that while these included the very best California offerings there were also some outstanding French estates and vintages.

He accepted a glass of champagne and settled into his new seat. It was kind of them to invite him into First Class, he thought; they were probably trying to make amends for the insult which had been offered him before boarding. Well, he was not one to bear a grudge, and he would overlook all that in the face of such a fulsome apology. He turned to look out of the window. It was a moonlit night, and they were over a sea of cloud; by pressing his face against the window he could just make out a field of stars above. How exhilarating it was to fly in such comfort, suspended between the silver-white of the clouds and the darkness above; and to be in the First Class cabin too – a tiny cocoon of Waterford crystal glasses, excellent wines and luxury foods, all kept in mid-air suspension by the very finest American technology.

Fatty looked into his glass of champagne, which was almost empty, and thought of the wines that lay ahead of him when they brought him his sumptuous first class meal, served on real porcelain. Would they offer him a Mouton Rothschild Premier Grand Cru? If not, it would be something close enough to that in quality. He thought for a moment of Betty, languishing in her narrow economy seat; it was such a pity she could not join him in First Class. Still, she would not appreciate fine wines quite as much as he would and she would be happy enough with those cheap plastic bottles they served back there.

As he was reflecting, the attendant brought him his tray. Fatty looked down at it, and then looked up at the attendant in mute incomprehension. Before him was a small, compartmentalised dinner tray of economy food (prawn cocktail; lasagne; chocolate mousse), all crammed together, with an upturned plastic beaker for the quarter bottle of Napa Valley Chardonnay which he had been unilaterally allocated.

It took him a few moments to recover his speech. Then he said indignantly: "Excuse me, but this is First Class. I'd like to see the menu, if you don't mind."

The attendant pursed her lips. "Sorry, sir, but you're actually an economy passenger. You've just been allocated here for seating purposes."

Fatty gasped. "But that's not fair!" he protested. "The food goes with the seat. You can't expect me to sit here and watch everybody else have all that fine food while you serve me this ... this fodder."

The attendant was unperturbed. "Those are the rules, sir. I'm very sorry. May I recommend our frequent flyer programme that allows you to build up points that can be used for upgrading tickets? I'll get you the leaflet if you wish."

Fatty pushed the tray away from him. "I'm not hungry," he said peevishly. "Take it away. And I don't want your leaflet either."

An hour or so later, when the other passengers were preparing for their Stilton and port, Fatty succumbed to the gnawing pains of hunger that had been becoming ever more insistent since he rejected his meal. Rising to his feet, he made his way towards the washroom; that at least, they would allow me to use, he thought. But he did not reach it; noticing that the attendants were busy with an elderly passenger at the front of the cabin who was having difficulty adjusting his seat, Fatty walked past the washroom and into the galley. There, laid out temptingly on their separate plates, were several slices of choice roast beef and half a smoked salmon. Wasting no time, he seized the salmon and tore off a large section, which he stuffed into his mouth. Then, snatching an open bottle of wine – and it was Mouton Rothschild after all – he took a deep swig. Then there was time for more smoked salmon and a quick slice or two of roast beef.

"Mr O'Leary?' It was the unhelpful attendant.

Fatty spun round, his mouth full of illicit food.

"That's first class food, Mr O'Leary," said the attendant severely. "You have no right to eat it."

Fatty tried to mumble an explanation, wanting to say that he was hungry and that he had not asked to be transferred to First Class and that it was quite invidious to make a distinction between himself and the others. But the explanation, had he managed it, would have fallen on deaf ears, as the attendant had by now summoned the

First Class purser and they were discussing the case in low tones. Fatty heard a few phrases as he munched on the last morsels in his mouth.

"Put him back there … Bring those other two up and put them here … Not the sort …"

His fate was revealed to him as tactfully as possible. He was to move back to his original seat and his two former neighbours would be transferred to First Class.

"Well at least you should warn them that they won't be getting any of the benefits," Fatty said sarcastically as he gathered his belongings for his ignominious return. But in that respect he was wrong. Twenty minutes later, when Fatty returned to retrieve his copy of *Antique Furniture Review*, inadvertently left in the First Class cabin, he saw his two former companions enjoying a full First Class meal, laid out before them on sparkling white porcelain. And each, he noticed, had a full glass of Mouton Rothschild.

Fatty returned to his seat, smarting at the injustice. Why should they be given treatment that had been denied him? What was it about them that made them worthy of a First Class meal while he was so cruelly and insensitively deprived? He looked out of his narrow economy window; the stars seemed to have disappeared and he could no longer see the clouds. And at that melancholy moment, the answer came to him. There was only one explanation, he thought. They were thin.

MAIN COURSE

A Taste of the Old Country

4

IRELAND CO-OPERATED, AT LEAST IN respect of its weather. At the moment that Fatty O'Leary's plane touched down on the runway of Shannon Airport, the morning sun burst through the clouds in glorious shafts of light, bathing the surrounding landscape with gold. Fatty did not mention to Betty the humiliations of the flight; it did not seem appropriate to mar with thoughts of recrimination this long-awaited moment of homecoming – for that is how Fatty viewed his first, tentative steps on Irish soil – a return home after a mere two generations of absence. So to Betty's questions as to whether he had been comfortable and whether he had enjoyed his dinner, he merely replied in the positive; it had all, he said, gone very quickly.

For whatever reason he immediately felt different, like a man with little or no past – a man poised on the brink of some immense self-discovery. Even in these first few minutes, it seemed to him as if something portentous was going to happen and that a new future was about to reveal itself. Of course it was just an airport, like any other, but the world beyond it was certainly different from the north Texas plains surrounding the terminal at Dallas: through a large plate-glass window he could already glimpse, in the distance beyond the low hills, the presumed green turf of those *Ur'*Learys.

Waiting for their luggage to appear on the carousel, the passengers stood in that odd half-intimacy of those who have been brought together for a journey, who recognise one another, dimly, but who are now once again becoming strangers. Suddenly the bags began to emerge from the mouth of some subterranean hall, as if being pushed up from the caverns of Lethe itself. Fatty spotted Betty's distinctive blue suitcase, and hauled it on to a trolley. Then came a succession of other bags, some similar in appearance to Fatty's, but none of them actually his.

"Perhaps there's a second load," said Betty helpfully, but Fatty, with sinking heart, knew that there never was a second consignment of suitcases. If a suitcase failed to appear, it was lost.

He sought out a man in uniform, who listened sympathetically before directing him to a small office. This, like an office of lost souls, had the air of a place of no hope. A chart was produced, with pictures of ownerless archetypical suitcases, like a police notice featuring delinquent or dangerous luggage; if suitcases could scowl, then these did. Fatty identified one that looked similar to his.

"It's a green suitcase with a black handle," he said. "And there's a label on it saying CORNELIUS O'LEARY, *Fayetteville, Arkansas.*"

The official wrote this down on a form, shaking his head slightly.

"That's a very common type of suitcase, that is," he said. "Those ones often go missing."

Fatty raised an eyebrow. "I don't see how the type of suitcase affects the chance of losing it," he said.

The official laughed. "Don't you believe it," he retorted. "In my line of work, you get a feeling for suitcases. And I'm telling you, your sort of suitcase goes missing: the number of suitcases like that I've had to try to trace, I couldn't begin to tell you. Where they all go I have no idea. Don't ask me."

Fatty was silent for a moment. This was a man who clearly knew the errant ways of suitcases. "You mean they never turn up?"

The official looked at him with rheumy eyes, his manner becoming more sympathetic as he realised that bad news would have to be broken. "I'm afraid that's a distinct possibility, sir. Still, if you tell me where you're staying, we'll deliver it to you if it ever turns up. What was in it by the way?"

"All my clothes," said Fatty miserably. "Everything I need."

The official shook his head. "Now that's a terrible thing," he said.

He tore off a strip of paper and handed it to Fatty. "That's your receipt," he said. "If you wish to make any enquiries, you must quote that number. That's a missing suitcase number."

Fatty pocketed his receipt and returned to Betty. He told her of what had happened and for a few moments they stood disconsolately, as if defeated by this fresh set-back. Ireland, which had seemed so rich in possibilities, now seemed like anywhere else: a place littered with snares and disappointments, a place where suitcases disappeared without trace.

"It's not the end of the world," said Betty eventually. "We'll go the hotel. We'll be able to wash and dry the clothes you're wearing while you have a rest. Then we'll go out and buy you some clothes to be getting on with." She paused. "Donegal tweeds, maybe."

Betty's ability to remain calm in a crisis was one of the qualities that most endeared her to Fatty. Her suggestion seemed to make a situation of dire discomfort quite bearable, and with a renewed sense that the trip could work out well, Fatty accompanied his wife to their hired car and set off on the relatively short journey to their destination. The weather still held, and his spirits rose as they left the airport and drove off along the winding road to Balinderry, on the southern side of Lough Derg.

They had booked themselves into Mountpenny House, a country house hotel that Fatty had read about in a guide to the fine Irish hotels. "On the shores of Lough Derg," the guide had enthused, "within yards of the lapping waters of this great, Shannon-fed lake, stands an oasis of tranquillity in a timeless countryside. Once a shooting lodge, its great rooms still echo to the sound of a thousand long-lost conversations over a log-fire. And in the dining room, where those weekend guests of old sat down to a breakfast of generous plates of kedgeree from silver platters, or tackled broad, well-smoked kippers, today's guests do just the same …"

"Oh," Fatty had said to Betty. "Did you see that? Kedgeree and kippers!"

For a moment he had pictured himself in some imagined Mountpenny House, engaged in conversation with a couple of other guests – perhaps *literati* from Dublin, who would quote from Shaw as intimately as if they knew him, and who would ask Fatty about Fayetteville and the theatre there, and Fatty would reply with a trenchant comment about the latest play. (What was the latest play? Fatty wondered. Was it something by Tennessee Williams, or was it Edward Albee? Were Williams and Albee dead? There was a presumption that dramatists were dead if they were at all well-known, but one could never be sure.) And then, the *bons mots* still hanging in the air, together they would proceed to dinner, laughing as they made their way along the corridor. At the table Fatty would regale his new Irish friends with stories of commodes and washstands, and there would be a fire in the grate casting its light on the heavy silver cutlery and the glistening crystal.

Now they were making their way up the driveway of the real Mountpenny House, through a thick wood that pressed in on either side. After half a mile of this, the wood gave way to a clearing and there, surrounded by lawns that rolled down to the lough-side, was the house itself. It was exactly what they had been promised in that effusive brochure, and more.

"This is the place," said Fatty proudly. "There's no doubt about it."

They parked the car and Fatty carried the single

suitcase in through the front door. Inside, a comfortable hall, furnished with boot-scrapers and pictures of horses, gave the visitor the impression that this was indeed what it appeared to be – a country house that happened to take visitors. On the table, on which there stood open a large, leather-covered visitors' book, there was an old brass bell button, which Fatty pushed tentatively. Somewhere in the kitchen, they heard a ringing sound.

Mrs Maeve O'Connor, the proprietrix, welcomed them warmly and took them up to their bedroom.

"We're a small place, as you know," she said, wiping her hands on her apron. "There are only six other guests at the moment. Next week's a bit busier. We have horse sales coming up and people are travelling down from Dublin, you know."

Mrs O'Connor showed them to their room and listened sympathetically while they told her about the loss of Fatty's suitcase. Betty asked whether it would be possible to wash his clothes so that he would not have to spend his first day in Ireland in the outfit in which he had travelled. This, said Mrs O'Connor, would be perfectly in order. There was a washing machine and a dryer in the small room off the scullery, and Betty was welcome to use them.

Fatty, who had not slept on the plane, now confessed to feeling very tired. Betty offered to wash his clothes for him while he tried to get a few hours' sleep; if he slept until early afternoon they would have time to go for a walk or even drive into the nearby village of Balinderry before dinner. He took a quick glance out of the window before disrobing. They were at the front of the house, and had an unimpeded view of the lawns running down to the lough. He noticed a small jetty, at which a rowing boat bobbed; beyond that, the great expanse of water and a distant shore of hills. He opened the window and drew a deep breath of air. It was slightly scented, the smell of gorse in flower, and it reminded him of an exhilarating spring morning in the hills back home.

Betty took his clothes and Fatty slipped into bed. Within a few minutes, his head full of satisfying thoughts about Ireland, he drifted off to sleep, lulled by the soporific sound of cattle lowing somewhere in the distance.

Betty found the laundry with little difficulty and loaded Fatty's clothes into the machine. Then, noticing that the wash would take forty minutes, she went outside, and took a walk along a path that meandered through the woods. She, too, was tired, but wanted to stay awake until evening, if possible, in order to get a good night's sleep.

And besides, she had never been abroad before and this first experience of a foreign country – or a foreign *home*, really – was too novel and exciting to sleep through. She found it hard to believe that the earth beneath her feet was Irish earth; that the trees were Irish trees; and that the rabbit which suddenly bounded off, giving her such a fright when she disturbed it in its foraging, was an Irish rabbit. At least she had no need to worry about snakes; St Patrick had seen to them all those years ago and the snakes, quite conscientiously, had strictly observed his edict since then. Of course snakes were part of Creation, and one might assume that somebody like St Francis would have been able to communicate with them; but one had to remind oneself about the all-embracing nature of Creation and remember that everything had its purpose in this life.

She sometimes wondered what was her own purpose in life. A husband or a wife can fill vast tracts of time in a life; Fatty was the focus of much of her thoughts; Fatty, that good, kind man who had saved her from what would have been a limited life in Mobile, Alabama, had opened her eyes to broader possibilities; Fatty, who always listened so courteously to her opinion even when she had to struggle to find the right word to express her thoughts; Fatty, who took so well the humiliations which the world

41

seemed to heap, so unfairly, on his generous shoulders. He was a great man and the finest husband a woman could hope to find. He was her purpose, and she liked to think that she was his. That surely was enough.

She reached the edge of the lough, coming across an old boathouse. It was dark inside, and the two boats within were clearly little used. One, a small rowing boat covered in flaking grey paint, had been nested in by birds; the other had a fishing rod and fishing net sticking out of it and gave off a musty odour.

She looked at her watch. Fatty's clothes would be ready in a few minutes and she would need to put them in the dryer. So she retraced her steps along the path and made her way back to the laundry. The room was now in silence. The machine had stopped and the front was open.

She looked inside, thinking that somebody had come in and, discovering the cycle at an end, had opened the door. The machine was quite empty.

"Oh," said Betty. And then *Oh* again.

There was no sign of Fatty's clothes in the laundry, and then, when she found Mrs O'Connor in the kitchen, where she was chopping carrots, she professed to have no idea what might have happened.

"Are you sure you put them in?" Mrs O'Connor asked.

"Sometimes I think I've put things into the oven and then discover the thing in question sitting outside an hour later. Are you sure?"

"I'm sure," said Betty. "I put everything in and started the machine. Then I went for a walk."

"Very strange," said Mrs O'Connor. "One of the other guests must have taken them out by mistake. I'll go and knock on some doors and see if anybody can help us solve this little mystery."

She went off, leaving Betty to wait in the kitchen. A few minutes later she returned, shaking her head.

"Nobody's in,' she said. "We'll have to wait until this evening and then ask around. I'm sure they'll turn up."

After a final, fruitless look around the laundry, Betty trudged upstairs to their room and opened the door gently. Fatty was still in bed, but as she came in he opened his eyes and smiled at her.

"Are they done?" he said. "I can't wait to get going."

Betty sat down on the edge of the bed and gently told him of what had happened.

"Then I have nothing at all to wear," he said despairingly. "I've now got no clothes at all."

Betty could think of nothing to say. It was difficult to know what to advise somebody who had no clothes.

43

What could such a person do?

"Well," said Fatty at last. "I suppose that we'll have to find a shop and buy some clothes."

Betty agreed, but asked how Fatty could get to the shop if he had nothing to wear. They had taken the car in Fatty's name and she could not drive it, so she could not go shopping by herself.

"I shall have to improvise," said Fatty, looking about him. He hoped to see a bathrobe hanging on the back of the door, but there was nothing. And the towels, although crisp and freshly-laundered, were decidedly too small to wrap round him.

"What about the quilt cover?" Betty asked after a few moments. "We could cut a hole for your head and arms up at the top and your legs could go through the slit at the other end."

Fatty was doubtful, but realised that there was no other possibility. He would willingly have donned Betty's clothes for the purpose of the expedition, but although she was generously built, he was even more so, and he knew that they would not fit.

Using her travel scissors, Betty cut a neat circular hole at the top of the cover, with two further holes at each side, one for each arm. Then, lifting the billowing white

44

garment over Fatty's head, she slipped it down over his body, to envelop him like a voluminous toga, or wheat sack, or collapsed parachute perhaps. Fatty did not look at himself in the mirror, but slicked back his hair and slipped on his shoes. Then, preceded by Betty, he made his way down the stairs with as much dignity as his unusual garb would allow.

Nobody saw them get into the car, and they were soon on the road to Balinderry, with Fatty at the wheel, berobed in white like a spectre. After they had driven down the one and only street, finding no shops that appeared to sell clothes, they consulted the map and continued to Nenagh, some distance away. There they pulled up outside the premises of Joseph Delaney and Sons, Outfitters (since 1938). The window display, at least, was promising. Alongside green waxed shooting jackets, clearly proof against the Irish elements, there were shirts and trousers and a large selection of tweed caps.

They waited until there were no passers-by in the immediate vicinity before they alighted from the car and made their way into the shop. There, if Mr Delaney was surprised to see Fatty dressed in a large white cover, he certainly did not show it, but greeted him as if he were wearing nothing unusual.

"I've lost my clothes," explained Fatty. "I need a whole new set."

Mr Delaney smiled. "Then you are certainly in the right place," he said. "I sell every sort of garment. Now, what size would you be in the waist and the collar departments? Then we can go from there."

As Fatty gave his measurements, Mr Delaney's face fell.

"Now isn't that a terrible thing?" he said, shaking his head. "Those sizes are all outsize. I don't think I go up that far."

There was silence. Fatty fingered the edge of his quilt cover despondently.

"But," continued Mr Delaney, "I cannot let a man who has lost his clothes go out of my shop with nothing to put on his back. I cannot do that, indeed no. We shall see what we can do about letting some items out. I can do that right here on the premises."

The outfitter set to with the taking of further measurements. There was an anxious moment when his tape measure proved inadequate, but this was soon remedied when he tied two measures together. "We'll just add the inches together," he said to Fatty.

Fatty sighed, and Mr Delaney paused, looking sympathetically at his customer. "Yes," he said gently.

"The world is not an easy place, is it now?"

Fatty looked up at the ceiling. It was not; it never had been.

"You could go and wait in the pub next door," Mr Delaney went on. "It's Delaney's too – another Delaney altogether, of course. Why don't you go and have a drink and a bite to eat while I do the necessary? You'll be more comfortable there if you ask my opinion on the matter."

Fatty was a little reluctant to venture into a bar while dressed in a quilt cover, but Mr Delaney assured him that nobody would think anything of it.

"They wear all sorts of things round here," he said. 'You should see how some of the fellows dress! You won't stand out at all."

Encouraged by this advice, Fatty and Betty pushed open the door of Terence Delaney's Saloon and walked up to the bar. Apart from the bartender, there was only one other person in the room, a thin-faced man with a large ginger moustache. He was seated at a stool at the bar, and he flashed them a broad smile as they entered.

"Good afternoon to you," he said. "It's a grand afternoon to be out. And a grand afternoon for a drink, so it is." He looked down at his empty glass. Fatty immediately took the cue and ordered drinks not only for himself and

Betty, but also for their fellow customer.

"Now that's very civil of you," said the man. "My name is Delaney, but not the Delaney who owns this bar. The Good Lord has been kind to me, but not that kind. Perhaps in the next life I shall own a bar, but alas that is not given to me in this present existence."

They sat down together at the bar while the drinks were being poured. Delaney had asked for both a pint of stout and a large Irish whiskey – "they go terribly well together," he had explained. "It's an awful pity to keep them apart, I always think."

They raised their glasses in a toast.

"Now you two good people are clearly Americans," said Delaney. "Judging from your outfits."

Fatty looked down at his quilt cover. "There's a reason for this ..." he began. But Delaney had more to say.

"We have many of our people in America," he said. "This part of Ireland played a big role in building up your country, so it did. Mr Lincoln. Mr Washington. Mr Eisenhower. All of them Tipperary men, I understand."

He raised his stout and took a deep draught, virtually draining the glass.

"Now you good people," he continued, "you are clearly from this part of the world too. Way back. I can tell."

Fatty beamed. "Do you think so? Well, I suppose that everywhere has its own look …"

"Of course it does," agreed Delaney. "Now would you look at that poor glass! Empty already!"

Fatty ordered another pint of stout and a further whiskey for their new friend.

"That's very good of you," said Delaney. "It helps me to talk about the old days in these parts. A spot of lubrication always helps." He paused, gulping at the stout. "Now then, where was I? You people are obviously from America. But let me guess which part. Boston?"

Fatty shook his head. "Fayetteville."

"Fattyville?" asked Delaney, wiping the foam from his moustache.

"No," said Fatty. "Fayetteville, Arkansas."

"Well now," said Delaney. "A lot of people went over from here to Arkansas. Back in the old days. A lot of people. What would your name be?"

"O'Leary," said Fatty.

Mr Delaney put his empty glass down with a thump. "O'Leary? Would you believe that? What a co-incidence, and the Good Lord himself is my witness." He looked ruefully at his empty glass before continuing. "I could have some very interesting information for you."

Fatty signalled to the barman. "A double here for Mr Delaney, please."

"Now that's very kind of you," said Delaney. "You see, my old grandfather knew an O'Leary who went over to America. Over to Fattyville, I think."

"Fayetteville."

"Yes, that's where he went."

Fatty looked at Betty. This was a marvellous development – very much better than they had dared hope. To get some actual information about the family roots – and so soon after arriving!

"My grandfather left Ireland in 1910," said Fatty. "He sailed from Cork, but came from these parts."

"Well," said Delaney. "That's exactly where my old grandfather said his friend O'Leary left from. Cork. And 1910 would be about right. Well, isn't that an amazing thing?"

The empty glass was moved slightly on the counter, and Fatty signalled to the barman again.

"What did he tell you?" asked Fatty. "What did he say?"

Delaney raised the drink to his lips. "He said that his friend O'Leary was a very fine fellow. A darling man. Just the best. That's what he said."

Fatty beamed at Betty. "You hear that Betty?'

"I did, Fatty."

Delaney looked down into his drink, as if to find further information in the glass.

"He had a farm, I think, somewhere in Tipperary, if I remember correctly. Quite near here, I think."

Fatty waited for further information, but none came.

"Well, isn't that wonderful," he said at last. "To find somebody with links with my family."

"Maybe closer than you think," said Delaney warmly. "You see, my mother was an O'Leary, would you believe it? And unless I'm mistaken, that makes me some sort of cousin to yourself."

For a moment Fatty did not know what to say. To find a cousin on the first day of his Irish trip seemed a quite exceptional stroke of luck. At this point, however, the barman intervened.

"That's enough of that, Paddy," he said to Delaney. "I think you should be heading off home now."

Delaney looked hurt. "Now, Micky, why would you be saying that? I'm enjoying a conversation with my friend Mr O'Leary."

"Yes, I've heard it all," said the barman. "And it's time for you to get home to your wife. Do you want me to be giving her a call?"

The offer was a threat, and Delaney picked up his hat.

"It's been a very great pleasure, Mr and Mrs O'Leary," he said. "And I do hope that we shall meet again some time soon. In more congenial surroundings, perhaps."

The barman watched him leave and then turned to Fatty. "Not a bad fellow, all in all," he said. "But he does tell the most terrible lies."

"So this business about being a cousin?" asked Betty.

"Probably not true, Mrs O'Leary," said the barman gently. "But here's a co-incidence. My mother's uncle, he was an O'Leary from Balinderry …"

They bought the barman a drink while they discussed the possibilities of being related. Then Fatty looked at his watch and realised that his clothes would be ready. They bade farewell and made their way out of the bar.

Mr Delaney had the clothes laid out on a table.

"Now, here we have a pair of trousers," he said. "I've let these ones out in one or two places and unpicked a few seams. And these shirts should be fine as long as you don't do up the top three buttons. And here's a jacket, which won't do up but the weather's nice and warm at the moment and that won't be a drawback. And socks and all the usual underwear and what have you. You'll be quite the lad in all these clothes, Mr O'Leary."

Fatty retired into the fitting room and came out in his new outfit, the duvet cover neatly folded over his arm. Mr Delaney fussed around him for a few moments, checking the garments, and then pronounced himself satisfied.

They paid and returned to the car to begin their drive back to Mountpenny House.

"Good can come from bad," said Betty. "If we hadn't lost your suitcase, then we wouldn't have met all those delightful people."

"Cousins too," said Fatty.

"Possibly," said Betty.

Then a thought occurred to Fatty.

"What about the quilt cover?" he asked. "You're going to have to tell Mrs O'Connor that we've cut holes in her quilt cover."

Betty reflected for a moment. "Why me?" she asked.

5

DINNER AT MOUNTPENNY HOUSE WAS preceded by the serving of drinks in the east drawing room. There, around a log fire set in the wide stone fireplace, the guests would assemble before dinner, exactly as had been promised in the brochure. Fatty and Betty were first down, Betty wearing the diaphanous silk dress she had brought with her for just such an occasion, Fatty wearing his new pants, which were a brown, houndstooth check, one of the green shirts prepared for him by Mr Joseph Delaney, and the jacket which did not do up. The overall effect, he thought, was not inappropriate. It was sufficiently casual for one who was on vacation and yet smart enough for a summer dinner party.

"You look so good, Fatty," Betty said, her voice lowered in deference to the refined atmosphere of the drawing room.

Fatty smiled. "Thanks to Mr Delaney. I wonder what happened to my clothes, though. I was fond of that shirt."

Betty shook her head. "You feel so helpless when abroad. Back home I would make no end of a fuss, but here you never know." She spoke with the air of one accustomed to overseas travel, and Fatty thought her observation quite pertinent. He himself had been to France before his marriage and he knew all about the perils of other cultures. He had also been to London on more than one occasion for antique shows and had come across the English and their curious ways; such strange people, and so utterly disconcerting.

They seated themselves on either side of the fire. Although it was early summer, the evenings were still cool, and there was a slight chill in the east-facing room. Fatty cast an eye round the room, appraising the contents. At one end of the room stood a double-fronted Victorian bookcase, stocked, he suspected, with books of a hunting and fishing nature; at the other was a grand piano (badly damaged casing, he thought) and a bureau on which a large occasional lamp (Chinese base, later Ching) had been placed. There were also several low tables, an Edwardian revolving bookcase, and an interesting Canterbury. The Canterbury, which was oak, with bronze fittings, was filled with magazines, and he and Betty each picked one out to read while they waited.

Fatty's choice was a recent copy of the glossy social magazine, *The Irish Tatler*. He paged through the advertisements for soft furnishings and Scotch whisky, past an article on the plans of the Irish Georgian Society, and alighted on one of the several social pages. This was interesting material. There had been a ball in County Wicklow, to which the social correspondent had gone. There was an account of the host's house – Strawberry Gothic in style "with a charming, quite charming" ballroom and minstrels' gallery. There were pictures of the guests, and a photograph of a long table groaning with salmon and game. Fatty thought that it looked as if it had been splendid fun, and for a moment he felt a pang of jealousy. That was a life that he could so easily be living, but would probably never experience. He knew nobody in County Wicklow; indeed the only people he knew in Ireland were the various Mr Delaneys, and he suspected that they moved in rather different circles from those portrayed in the social columns of *The Irish Tatler*.

He turned the page. There had been a reception in Dublin to mark the opening of a new art gallery. According to the magazine, *everybody* had been there. And there they were, photographed talking to one another over glasses of wine. *Professor Roderick Finucane* of Trinity College was seen talking to *Miss Georgina Farrell* and her aunt, the well-known water-colourist, *Mrs Annabel Farrell*, recently returned from *Bermuda*. Then there was conversation between *Mr Pears van Eck* and *Mr Maurice Shaw*, both of them directors of the *Irish Foundation for the Fine Arts*, neither of them the sort that one finds in Arkansas, thought Fatty. Beneath that photograph was a slightly larger picture of *Mr Rupert O'Brien*, the well-known critic, his wife, *Mrs Niamh O'Brien*, the successful actress, currently appearing (as Juno) in *Juno and the Paycock* at the Abbey Theatre, and His Excellency, the Italian Ambassador to Ireland, *Mr Cosimo Pricolo*, all sharing what appeared to be a most amusing joke. Fatty studied the photographs carefully. What was it about these people that made their lives seem so much more exotic and exciting than his own? He glanced at Betty, sunk in a copy of *Horse and Hound*. He wondered what he and Betty would look like on the social pages of *The Irish Tatler*. He allowed his mind to wander: *Mr and Mrs Cornelius O'Leary at Mountpenny House in County Tipperary. Mr O'Leary, a noted antique dealer, is in Ireland to purchase fine Irish furniture for the American market. His wife, the daughter of a well-known Mobile real-estate broker ...*

Fatty's thoughts were interrupted by the entry into the room of a group of fellow guests, two women and a diminutive man in a tweed suit. The women, who looked sufficiently similar to be sisters, smiled at Betty and the small man gave a nod in Fatty's direction. They moved over to the piano and one of the women self-consciously sat at the keyboard and ran her fingers over the keys.

"Play us a tune, Ella," said the other woman.

"Go on," said the man. "Satie. You do Satie so well, and everybody likes Satie."

The woman at the piano blushed. "I would not inflict myself …" she began.

Fatty rose to his feet. 'It would be no infliction, M'am," he said. "My wife and I like Satie very much."

The woman looked down at the keyboard and began to play.

"Ah," said Fatty, contentedly. *"The Gymnasium."*

They listened raptly – so raptly indeed that they did not notice others coming into the room. Only after the limpid notes had died away did Fatty look up and see that another couple had entered and taken a seat on the sofa by the fire. He looked at them for a moment, before turning to congratulate the pianist. But a vague sense of familiarity made him turn back and look again.

The man, who was wearing an elegant, double-breasted suit and a subdued red tie, had a look of distinction about him. The woman, who was dressed in a dark trouser suit, had high cheekbones and almond eyes. Fatty had seen them before; he was sure of it.

"Thank you so much," the man called out to the

pianist. "A *gymnopédie* before dinner. A perfect start to the evening. I feel quite limbered-up!'

The woman laughed. "You play so well, my dear. Why don't you continue?"

"Because I need a drink," said the woman at the piano.

At this point Mrs O'Connor came in, wheeling a drinks trolley on which an array of bottles was placed. She looked round, as if counting her guests, and then announced that drinks would be served.

"Mr O'Brien, I've taken the trouble to get you your usual," she said to the man on the sofa. "You made me feel so ashamed last time – not having it in the house."

"You spoil me, Mrs O'Connor," said the elegant man. "If you're not careful, I'll never stop coming here. You'll not be able to get rid of us. We'll move in permanently. We'll *live* with you!"

"I don't think that the *Irish Times* would like that," said the hostess, pouring a large measure of gin into a glass. "Nor the Abbey Theatre, for that matter."

Fatty listened, fascinated. They spoke so easily, exchanging this subtle repartee as if they were uttering the lines of a play. But it was the mention of the Abbey Theatre that triggered the memory, and it came to him so suddenly that he almost gasped. Of course he had seen this couple before; they were Rupert and Niamh O'Brien, and he had seen their picture in the *Irish Tatler*. Rupert O'Brien, the critic, and his wife, Niamh, the famous actress (recently Juno in *Juno and the Paycock*).

Mrs O'Connor served the drinks and then withdrew, announcing that dinner would be in twenty minutes.

Rupert O'Brien sat back on the sofa.

"Bliss," he announced to the room at large. "A whole weekend ahead of us with no telephone."

Fatty plucked up the courage to say something.

"No telephone," he remarked.

Rupert O'Brien glanced in his direction briefly and then looked at the others.

"Such a peaceful place," he said. "Such intriguing shades of the past."

What did that mean? Fatty wondered. Did it merely suggest that the house was old, in which case why was that intriguing?

Taking a sip of his gin and tonic, he plucked up his courage again. After all, why should he not contribute to the discussion? If Rupert O'Brien could say something about the house, then he could too.

"How old is this house?" he ventured.

There was a silence. The pianist and her party looked

at one another, but said nothing.

"Quite old, I suspect," said Betty. "We have nothing this old in Arkansas."

"Oh it's not old at all," said Rupert O'Brien airily. "Late Victorian. Lamb dressed up as mutton, so to speak."

"That's quite old," said Betty. "In the United States everything is much newer. Victorian is pretty old."

"Age is relative, of course," said Rupert O'Brien. "Our children regard us as terribly old. But I'm not old at all."

"How old are you?" asked Betty pleasantly.

The silence that resulted seemed cold.

"I wonder if there are fish in the lake," Fatty said hurriedly.

Everybody looked at him.

"Vast numbers, I suspect," said Rupert O'Brien, still glaring at Betty. "Young fish, old fish ..."

"Well," said the pianist cheerfully. "They're under no threat from me. I have never succeeded in catching a fish in my life. Not one."

"I caught a big fish last month," Fatty chipped in. "My friend Tubby O'Rourke and I went up to one of the lakes in the north of our state and I caught a very large fish. Tubby caught quite a few, but none of them very large. I think he was using the wrong sort of fly."

"Oh," said Rupert O'Brien.

"It was delicious," said Betty. "I barbecued it. Fresh fish is delicious when barbecued with some lemon and butter."

Niamh now made her first contribution.

"Poor fish. I do feel so sorry for them. One moment in those gorgeous watery depths and the next moment in the cruel air, gasping for breath."

"Oh I don't know, my dear," said Rupert O'Brien. "I expect that fish would catch us, if they could. One mustn't romanticise nature. I'm for Darwin rather than Ruskin. Survival of the fishes, you know."

He burst out laughing, and Fatty, although he did not take the reference, immediately joined in.

"Ha!" said Fatty. "Ruskin!"

At this point the pianist sat down and began to play determinedly. This ended the conversation until Mrs O'Connor returned to call them in for dinner.

6

It was the custom at Mountpenny House for all the guests to dine together at one large table, as they would do if they were weekend guests in a country house. Individual tables were allowed at breakfast, when the desire to make conversation might be expected to be less pressing; and again weekend guests would have been expected to come down at different times.

Fatty and Betty were the first to go through, and established themselves in chairs near the window. They were followed by the pianist and her companions, who opted to sit at the other end of the table, leaving two vacant chairs next to Fatty and Betty. Thus when Rupert and Niamh O'Brien entered the room, they had no alternative but to sit next to Fatty and Betty.

Although there was no choice for dinner – the guests being required to eat what had been prepared – Mrs O'Connor still copied for each place an elegantly-written menu, which informed the guests of what lay ahead. Rupert O'Brien picked this up and read out to the table at large:

"Fish Soup, Mountpenny-style, my goodness, follow-ed by *Scaloppine alla Perugina*, and then apricot tart or chestnuts with Marsala. Wonderful!"

"I wonder what fish they put in the soup," said Betty.

"From the lough, I expect," said Rupert O'Brien. "Or perhaps from the sea. One never knows."

"No," said Fatty. "But either would be very satisfactory I'm sure."

"Mind you," Rupert O'Brien went on, "there are precious few fish left in the sea. Yeats was able to write a line about the 'mackerel-teeming seas of Ireland'. He wouldn't be able to do that today."

"What's happened?" asked Fatty.

"The Spanish have eaten them all," said Rupert O'Brien. He turned to Niamh. "How do you think they do their *scallopine*? Do you think it'll be the same way as they did them in that charming little hotel in Perugia? With croutons?"

"I expect so," said Niamh. "Such *mignon* croutons; small and *mignon*."

"Do you know Italy well?" asked Fatty.

"Tolerably," replied Rupert O'Brien. "Venice, Milan, Florence, Rome, Naples, Ravenna, Siena and Perugia. Oh, and Palermo too. But ignorant about the rest, I'm afraid. And you?"

"I plan to go there some time," said Fatty. "It's difficult

for us to get away from home. We've been waiting for this trip for some time."

"And tell me," said Rupert O'Brien, breaking his bread roll over his plate, "where would home be?"

"Fayetteville," replied Fatty.

"Fartyville?"

"Fayetteville," said Fatty. "Fayetteville, Arkansas."

"Oh," said Rupert O'Brien.

"Croutons," Niamh interjected. "They did use croutons. I remember now. And they served them with *crostini di fegatini*. We had them just before we were due to go off to Urbino."

"Of course," said Rupert O'Brien. "I remember that well. And we went to that marvellous little museum where they had the most surprising pictures. The Vincenzo Campi picture of the breadmaker, with all those marvellous loaves on the table and those perfectly angelic little children looking on while the baker dusted his hands with flour." He turned to Fatty. "You know it? That picture?"

Fatty appeared to think for a moment. "I don't think so. No, I don't think I do."

"Lovely textures," said Rupert O'Brien. "Lovely rich colours. Vibrant. Positively edible. You know, my test for art is this: *Do I want to eat it?* If I want to eat something, then I know it's good."

"That's a good test," said Fatty. He thought of washstands. Would it work for them as well?

"Mind you," said Rupert O'Brien, "mediocre paintings of food can confuse the test. You may want to eat them, but for the wrong reasons. Take Giovanna Garzoni, for instance. You'll know his picture of the Old Man of Artimino, of course. You know it?"

Fatty shook his head.

"Well it's a remarkable painting. It hangs in the Pitti Palace in Florence. You know the Pitti Palace?"

"No," said Fatty.

"But you know Florence, of course?" went on Rupert O'Brien.

Again Fatty shook his head.

"No matter," said Rupert O'Brien. "That's a mediocre painting of food. A lovely ripe melon, split open, a delicious-looking ham, a bird, some cherries, everything just asking to be eaten. But the composition is most peculiar, and the perspective is all over the place. In fact, it has an almost-Daliesque quality to it. Do you know Dali?'

"Yes," said Fatty, with relief. "I know Dali."

"Where did you meet him?" asked Rupert O'Brien.

"Oh," said Fatty. "I thought you meant …"

"I met him at his villa," went on Rupert O'Brien. "Pre-Niamh days, of course. She was just a snip of a thing at drama school then. I was in Barcelona for a couple of months and I was invited out to Dali's villa with some gallery friends. Peculiar place. Rather like …"

He was interrupted by the arrival of a young waitress, one of the girls from the village, who brought in the large bowls of fish soup.

"Gorgeous," said Rupert O'Brien, sniffing at his soup. "Just the right amount of garlic, I can tell. Never put too much garlic in your fish soup. Robin Maugham told me that. You know him? Famous writer. He learned all about garlic in the soup from his uncle, Willie Maugham – Somerset Maugham, you know. Great enthusiast *pour la table*. Maugham *neveu* used to visit his uncle at the Villa Mauresque, where he had a famous cook. People used to do anything for an invitation to luncheon with the old boy because of Madame *dans la cuisine*. Apparently she used to cook for the Pope, but became fed up with the all those goings-on in the Vatican and returned to France. Mind you, it's a bit of a waste of time placing fine food before a pope. They really are most unappreciative of the finer things in life. Most of them are pretty unsophisticated priests from remote villages with tastes to match. John XXIII was like that, I'm sorry to say. No understanding of art, I gather. None at all. Pius XII, may his blessed soul rest in peace, was the last pontiff of any breeding, you know. Terribly good family he came from; old Roman aristocrats. Mind you, he had a delicate stomach and could only eat polenta, poor fellow. Pity about his friendship with *il Duce*, but there you are."

Fatty dipped his spoon into his soup. He looked at Betty, who was watching anxiously to see which spoon was being used.

"Such a beast, Mussolini," said Rupert, between mouthfuls of soup. "Psychopathic braggart. And irredeemably *petit bourgeois*. I don't know which is worse, probably neither. Do you know that he tried to impress his people by performing so-called feats of bravery? He went into the lions' cage at Rome Zoo, just to show that he was unafraid. But the Italian press didn't say that they had drugged the lions and they couldn't have harmed a fly. It's all in that recent biography somebody brought out the other day. Frightful rubbish. Have you seen it?"

Fatty was silent. He had finished his soup, and would have liked to have more, but there was no tureen handy and he would have to wait until the next course was served before he could appease his appetite.

"Tell me," said Rupert suddenly. "What is your line of business Mr … Mr …"

"O'Leary," said Fatty.

"Mr O'Leary. What sort of business are you in?"

"Antiques," said Fatty.

"How interesting," said Rupert. "I pride myself on my own eye in that direction. I helped old Lord Balnerry sort his stuff out. You know his place? Down near Cork?"

"No," said Fatty, adding, quietly, "I don't seem to know anyone. Except Delaney, that is."

Rupert looked surprised. "Judge Delaney?" he said. "The Supreme Court man? You know him?"

"No," said Fatty. "Joseph Delaney, the tailor. He fixed me up when my clothes were lost."

"Well, there you are," said Rupert O'Brien. "Friends are useful. I remember I was in Miami once and I lost my jacket. But I bumped into Versace at a party and I told him, and he said: *Funny – I'm a tailor! I'll fix you up*. And he did, would you believe it?"

Fatty looked down at his plate, and then gazed at the houndstooth trousers that Mr Delaney had adjusted for him. They were made of cheap material and looked shabby beside the thick cloth of Rupert O'Brien's elegant suit.

"We're simple people in Arkansas, Mr O'Brien," Betty suddenly burst out. "But we do our best. And my husband is a good man. He always has been."

"I'm sure," said Rupert O'Brien smoothly. "I'm sure he is."

"And just because we don't mix in the sort of circles you mix in," she went on, "that doesn't mean to say that we don't amount to anything. We're still your company for the evening. We didn't ask to be, but we are. My husband is a good man. He may not have read everything or met everybody, but he's a good man. And in my book, that's what counts."

A complete silence had fallen over the table. Spoons, which had been dipped into soup, were stopped, poised half-way to trembling lips; nobody moved.

"So if you'll excuse us, Mr and Mrs O'Brien," said Betty. "We shall find somewhere quieter to have our dinner."

She rose to her feet and moved deliberately over to one of the unlaid tables at the other side of the room, taking her placemat and side-plate with her. Fatty, immobilised for a few moments, did nothing, but then, with an apologetic nod to the others, he too got up and went over to the other table.

"I'm sorry, my dear," whispered Betty. "I couldn't stand it any more. I just couldn't."

"That's all right," said Fatty, reaching over to place his hand on hers, his voice uneven. "I'm so proud of you. And anyway, I would sooner sit here and look at you any time, than listen to all his highfalutin' talk through dinner."

Betty smiled at him. She noticed that there were tears on his cheeks. She reached into her pocket and extracted a small, Irish linen handkerchief that Mr Delaney, the outfitter, had given her.

"Here," she said. "Use this."

They sat in silence at their separate table. After a few minutes, the waitress returned to clear away the soup plates and bring in the main course. This she placed unceremoniously on the table, leaving the guests to help themselves.

"All the more for us," said Rupert O'Brien, passing the serving spoon to Niamh. "Short rations for some, I'm afraid."

Fatty leant over the table to whisper to Betty. "Did you hear that, Betty? Did you hear what he said?"

Betty nodded, and they both watched miserably as the main course disappeared at the other table. There was no sign of the waitress and they both realised that there was nothing that they could do without losing face to a quite unacceptable extent.

"We shall simply withdraw," said Fatty, after a while. "I'm no longer hungry."

"And neither am I," said Betty.

But her voice lacked conviction.

Upstairs in their room, they retired to their beds, separated by a bedside table on which back issues of *Horse and Hound* and two glasses of water had thoughtfully been placed by Mrs O'Connor. They were both tired, and the light was put out almost immediately.

"Our first night in Ireland," said Betty, in the darkness.

"Yes," said Fatty. "I hope that tomorrow's a bit better."

"It will be, Fatty," said Betty. "It will be."

Fatty was silent. Then: "Betty, I felt so … so *inadequate* beside that O'Brien person. He made me feel so *small*."

"You're not small," said Betty.

"No," said Fatty. "I know."

He paused. "Come and lie beside me, Betty. Come and lie on my bed and hold my hand until I go to sleep, like you used to do when we were younger."

"Of course, my dear," said Betty, slipping out of her bed and lowering herself onto the space prepared by

Fatty, who had rolled over to one side of the bed.

"Dear Fatty …"

She did not complete her sentence. The bed collapsed.

7

MRS O'CONNOR WAS PERFECTLY UNDERSTANDING about the broken legs of the bed.

"These things happen," she said early the following morning, when Fatty sought her out in the kitchen to confess to the damage. "I remember, a few years ago, we had a couple of guests who … "

She paused, and Fatty waited expectantly.

"Who …" he prompted.

Mrs O'Connor said nothing. She had been wiping a surface when he entered the kitchen and now she resumed her task. He was watching her idly when, in a moment of shock, he realised that he recognised the pattern of the cloth. He was sure it was his shirt – or part of his shirt.

"My clothes," he muttered. "What happened to them?"

Mrs O'Connor shook her head and deliberately changed the subject. "Does Mrs O'Leary enjoy a cooked breakfast?" she asked.

"She does," replied Fatty emphatically.

"Kippers?" asked Mrs O'Connor.

"Oh yes," said Fatty. "I read about your kippers and kedgeree."

"There will be plenty of both," said Mrs O'Connor.

"Whenever you're ready, come down and have breakfast.

Fatty returned to the room to convey to Betty the news about breakfast. They were both ravenously hungry after their failed dinner the previous evening, and were looking forward to a substantial meal, at their own table. With any luck Rupert and Niamh O'Brien would not surface until much later; they did not seem the types to be up and about early. He imagined Rupert O'Brien in a silk dressing-gown, reading out his own column in the *Irish Times* to Niamh, who would also be clad in a silk dressing-gown and reclining in bed. The legs of their bed would be intact, too.

He frowned as he remembered the piece of cloth with which Mrs O'Connor had been wiping the kitchen table. Was it just a coincidence that it should have the same pattern as his shirt, or had she ... He stopped himself. It was an absurd idea: why would Mrs O'Connor steal his shirt and then cut it up to make cleaning cloths? No, however odd Ireland was, it was not *that* odd.

Since it would take Betty half an hour or so to get ready for breakfast, Fatty decided to run himself a bath. The bathroom, which seemed to have been untouched since Victorian days, was dominated by an immense iron bathtub, standing on clawed feet, and crowned at the deep end with glistening steel taps. At the top of each tap, set generously in ceramic, an ornate HOT and COLD enlightened one as to which tap was which. It was a museum piece of a bathtub, and Fatty was looking forward to sinking into a pool of steaming hot water, drawn, he imagined, from the sweet waters of the lough.

With a sigh of pleasure, Fatty sank into the tub, allowing the resultant waves to slop over the edge and on to the stone-flagged floor. The water was just as he had expected it: an embrace as soft as the Irish air from which it had originally fallen as rain. He closed his eyes and tried a few lines of song. Fatty, who had a passable singing voice, enjoyed Neapolitan *bel canto*, which he had taught himself from a collection of old records discovered in a cupboard he had bought. Now he sang his favourite, *Come facette mammetta? When your mother made you, how did she do it? To make your flesh, she took a hundred roses and milk, Concetta. For your mouth she used strawberries, honey, sugar and cinnamon, and for your hair, a whole chest of gold.*

The words of longing and admiration rose up to the ceiling of the bathroom. Inside the room, Betty smiled with pleasure; Fatty had explained to her that this song was, in his mind, about her; that she was his Concetta. She liked to hear Fatty singing, particularly after some moment of setback or trial. His singing on this particular morning was a sign that his spirits were undented by the difficulties of the previous day. And here they were, in the lush heart of Ireland, with the sun streaming in through their half-open window and a gentle, balmy breeze nudging the curtains.

Fatty luxuriated in the bath until the water began to cool. Now it was time for breakfast and he began to ease himself up. But he did not get far. He tried again, but his effort seemed only to wedge him further in. He was stuck in the bath.

He called out to Betty, who rose from the bed and padded into the bathroom.

"I seem to be stuck, Betty," moaned Fatty. "I can't move."

Betty rushed to his side and took hold of one of his arms.

"I'll give you a little tug, Fatty," she said. "That'll dislodge you. Don't worry."

She pulled at his arm, her hands slipping along Fatty's wet flesh. It seemed to make no difference.

"I'll pull out the plug," she said. "If the water drains out, it might make things easier."

It did not. Indeed, the absence of the water seemed

to lodge Fatty's hips even more firmly into the trap. Nor did soap, liberally applied to the side of the bath, seem to make any difference.

"It's hopeless, Betty," Fatty moaned. "Nothing seems to help. I'm just stuck."

Betty stood back and wiped her brow.

"I shall get you a towel," she said. "That will preserve your modesty while I call Mrs O'Connor."

Betty draped a towel across Fatty's midriff, donned her dressing-gown, and left the room. Once downstairs, she unsuccessfully sought their hostess in the kitchen, but found her at last in the dining room, leaning against a sideboard and engaged in conversation with the pianist from the previous evening. To her displeasure, she noticed that Rupert and Niamh O'Brien were already seated at a table in the window, tucking into large helpings of kedgeree. Rupert O'Brien looked up briefly from his plate, noticed Betty's dressing-gown, and gave a disapproving frown.

Mrs O'Connor could tell from Betty's expression that something was wrong.

"Not another bed problem," she said, with concern.

Hearing this, Rupert O'Brien raised an eyebrow.

"No," whispered Betty. "It's my husband. He's stuck

in the bath."

Rupert O'Brien dug his fork into his kedgeree with renewed vigour. Niamh looked out of the window, her hand at her mouth.

"Oh dear," said Mrs O'Connor. "What a terrible thing. I shall come up immediately."

They left the dining room and were soon confronting the unfortunate Fatty, still firmly lodged in the bath, a damp white towel across his middle.

"Good morning, Mr O'Leary," said Mrs O'Connor cheerfully. "This is a sad to-do, so it is."

"Good morning, Mrs O'Connor," Fatty replied. "I'm sorry about this. I can't move."

"We'll both give a wee tug,' suggested Mrs O'Connor, moving to the head of the bath. I'll pull on his feet here, Mrs O'Leary, and you can pull on his arms. The two of us might shift him, so we might."

The two women seized an extremity of Fatty and began to pull vigorously. But even their combined strength made no impression on the immobile Fatty, and after one or two further efforts, with much huffing and puffing, they abandoned their effort.

Mrs O'Connor thought for a few moments. "I'll call Delaney," she said after a while.

"Delaney?" asked Fatty.

'Yes," said Mrs O'Connor. "Delaney, the plumber. This is a job for a professional, I'm afraid. Delaney's just down the road. He'll be here in no time."

Delaney, with all the discretion of one who is professionally party to the most intimate problems of others, appeared to be not in the least surprised by Fatty's plight. He surveyed the problem from all angles, knocking on the side of the bath with his bare knuckles to determine where the obstruction lay. He, too, tried to dislodge Fatty by pulling at his arms, until Fatty gave a yelp of pain from the plumber's rough tug.

"I'm sorry, Mr O'Leary," he said. "But I'm going to have to remove the bath. I've got a device down in my workshop that will enable me to prise the bath open a bit and set you free. But I can't bring it in here, you see."

Fatty gazed at the plumber's ruddy face, with its chapped skin and eruption of subcutaneous warts around the nose. He opened his mouth to protest, and then closed it. What was the point? There seemed to be no other way of getting him free, and he could not spend much longer stuck in this cold, inhospitable couch.

"But don't you go worrying about it," said the

plumber. "I've freed people from baths before. You've got no idea how often it happens."

Reaching into the bag that he had carried in with him, he extracted several tools, with which he proceeded to remove the taps. That done, he unscrewed the ornamental clawed feet from their stone setting, and finally detached the drainpipe from the bottom of the tub.

"That's coming along very nicely," he said as he stood up to inspect his labours. "Now I'll just go down and get a few hands to help and we'll be on our way."

Fatty lay gloomily in his prison while the plumber summoned help. Ten minutes later Mr Delaney returned with the chef, a powerfully-built figure with rolled-up sleeves, and a man who had been tending cattle in a field at the edge of the lough.

"Right boys," said the plumber cheerily. "We'll just give this old bath a lift and carry it down the stairs to my van. One, two, three!"

Fatty felt himself being lifted into the air as his three straining porters began their slow journey down the stairs and out into the courtyard.

"We'll have you out of there in no time at all," said Delaney reassuringly, as they manoeuvred the bath out of the back door.

"Yes," said the cattleman, peering over the edge of the bath at Fatty. "It's an awful shame for a visitor like yourself to have this happen to him. An awful shame."

Fatty tried to smile, but it was difficult. He wondered whether he should try a trick that he had used as a young boy, whereby he closed his eyes and simply pretended that he was not there. If he did this now, he might be able to transport himself mentally back to his home in Fayetteville and imagine himself sitting on the deck with Betty. Or perhaps he could think of himself bowling with Tubby O'Rourke and Porky Flanagan, or even take himself back to boyhood and see himself fishing with his father in the lake near their summer-house. Such pleasant images, these were, but not strong enough to protect him from the intrusion of reality, for now he heard the cattleman give a shout and the bath began to be lowered slowly to the ground.

"Those wretched cows have broken through the gate again," the cattleman grumbled. "Could you come and give me a quick hand now to chase them back in before they get on to Mrs O'Connor's lawns and there's a real hullabaloo."

Fatty opened his eyes and stared up at a sky framed by the smooth white sides of the bathtub. Suddenly the plumber's face and torso loomed over the edge.

"Sorry about this, Mr O'Leary," he said. "We'll have to leave you here for a minute or two while we go and deal with those cows. You just wait now."

"What else can I do but wait?" said Fatty petulantly. "I can hardly go anywhere."

"Well, now, that's probably true," said the plumber. "But don't you worry. We'll be back in no time."

Fatty closed his eyes and tried again to imagine that this simply was not happening. Ever since he had set out for Ireland, he had been subjected to a series of misfortunes and humiliations, one after the other. There had been that awful flight, with all its indignities; there had been the embarrassment of having to wear a duvet cover into town; and then, last night, there had been the disaster with the bed. But all of these events, acutely embarrassing as they might have been, were nothing when compared with the sheer indignity of being dumped, covered only by a small towel, in the middle of the courtyard. Fortunately there was nobody about, although at any moment somebody might appear. What if that dreadful O'Brien person decided to take a stroll and walked out into the courtyard to find a large white bath tub, apparently abandoned, and Fatty stuck inside it at the mercy of any passer-by? Fatty stared up at the sky and uttered a small prayer to Saint Martha, the patron saint of cooks, and with a secondary patronage of the overweight, but, half way through, switched, quite wisely, to an appeal to St Eustace, patron saint of difficult situations. *Dear St Eustace, who wrought such wonders, please raise your faithful servant, CORNELIUS PATRICK O'LEARY, from his plight, and return him to his room in the hotel. Amen.* In the distance he heard vigorous shouts and calls coming from the men as they chased the cows; no immediate help would be forthcoming from that quarter, it seemed.

Fatty took a deep breath. Perhaps I should be entirely philosophical about this, he thought. Things can hurt us only if we allow them to hurt us; if we think of them as trials over which we can easily triumph, then their sting is drawn; so he had been taught, all those years ago at Notre Dame, when they had studied the Stoics. And matters could be worse. One only had to think of the sufferings of the saints to know that. They were subjected to the most terrible tortures and pains, and they bore them as if they were the lightest of glancing blows. He would do the same. To be stuck in a bath was nothing to the arrows that pierced Saint Sebastian, for example, or the kindled conflagration that consumed Saint Joan.

As he lay in silence, feeling the cold grasp of the bathtub, he heard the door into the courtyard open and the sound of footsteps.

"What on earth is that?" said a voice. With a sinking heart, Fatty recognised that the voice belonged to Rupert O'Brien.

The footsteps grew louder and there, peering over him, was the face of the famous critic, wide-eyed with surprise. Behind him, but taking only a quick glance before withdrawing from view, was the face of Niamh.

"Mr O'Leary! You poor fellow!"

Fatty grimaced. "I'm stuck," he said. "The plumber was taking me to his workshop and he had to go off and chase some cows. I can't move till they come back."

"But you poor fellow, what a shame," said Rupert O'Brien, stretching out to touch the side of the bath in sympathy. "They should not have deserted you like that. I shall stay here and talk to you. Niamh, you go back inside. It's embarrassing enough for Mr O'Leary to be out here with virtually no clothes without ladies being present."

"I'm quite all right," said Fatty hurriedly. "Don't worry about me."

"But of course I shall worry," said Rupert O'Brien,

perching himself on the edge of the bathtub. "I suppose you were too large for the bath. Is that what happened? Were you just too large?"

Fatty mumbled something that Rupert O'Brien did not hear. "I remember," went on Rupert O'Brien, "when I was at school – Campbell College, you know it? – we had a fellow who got stuck in an armchair. He was a large fellow, a bit like yourself but maybe not quite so large, and he sat in this armchair and he simply could not get out of it. His father was Irish Ambassador in Paris at the time, I distinctly remember. He was considered a possible president at one stage, but he was rather too fond of the ladies and you know what the bishops are like in this country. Frightful bunch of kill-joys. But anyway, there was his son, stuck in an armchair and no amount of pulling seemed to be able to do the trick. I thought one of the springs might have got hooked into him, you know, and this would have made it difficult to dislodge him. Then I had a good idea, which was to turn the armchair upside down and let gravity do the trick. So we did, and out he eventually popped, barely damaged by the whole experience, even if he did have a large rent in the seat of his pants, which gave us a good laugh. You know what boys are like. Cruel bunch. Ha!"

Fatty clenched his teeth in desperation. He was as captive an audience as those unfortunate Romans who were obliged to hear Nero play his fiddle and who could only escape the auditorium by pretending to die.

"Funny that," mused Rupert O'Brien. "We couldn't tug him out, but gravity, exercising its force in the opposite direction ..." He paused, and Fatty opened his eyes to see a thoughtful expression on the face of his unwelcome companion.

"My goodness, we could do the same for you," said Rupert O'Brien. "If I just roll this tub over, you'll be upside down and then you'll probably come out through the operation of gravity. Why didn't I think of it before?"

Fatty shook his head. "No," he protested. "They'll be back soon. Just leave me."

"Wouldn't hear of leaving you," said Rupert O'Brien. "Now, don't you worry. I'll just give this a bit of a push and you'll be over. Let me see, just here."

Fatty felt the bathtub rocking and then, with a sudden lurch, it toppled over onto its side. There was a ringing clang, like a deadened bell, and then the movement started again and he felt the bathtub roll once more.

"There!" shouted Rupert O'Brien. "That's it."

Fatty was now upside down, his view of the sky being

replaced with a dark view of the cobbled surface of the courtyard.

Rupert O'Brien tapped loudly on the bathtub. "Are you all right in there, Mr O'Leary," he shouted. "Are you beginning to slip out?"

"I am still caught," said Fatty miserably. "Turn it over again. I don't like being upside down. Just mind your own business."

"Now, now, Mr O'Leary," said Rupert O'Brien. "I can understand that you're upset, but this really is the only way. I'll stay and talk to you while gravity gets to work. What would you like to chat about? I'd like to be able to talk about that place you come from – what was it called – but I don't know a thing about it. I've never been there. I've been to New York, of course. I've been there a lot, in fact. Do you know that I used to write the occasional piece for the *New Yorker*? Do you read the *New Yorker*, Mr O'Leary? Can you buy it down in Mississippi? There are some who say that it's gone off and that the standards of grammar are not what they used to be. There may be some truth in that. What do you think? Do you think that the *New Yorker* has gone off at all?"

"Go away ..." Fatty started to shout, but was cut short by a sudden pain in his right hip, and then, to the accompaniment of a great sucking sound, like that made by a mud pool venting, he felt himself tumbling from the bath and onto the hard cobbles. He uttered a yell of pain and this brought an anxious enquiry from Rupert O'Brien.

"Has it worked? Are you out?"

Fatty, crouching beneath the bath, doubled up most uncomfortably, struggled to retrieve the towel, which had fallen from his waist when the bath had been turned over.

"I'm out now," he shouted. "Please turn the bath over again."

Fatty heard Rupert O'Brien breathing heavily as he exerted himself to roll the bathtub over on to its side, but eventually he succeeded, exposing Fatty, like an insect discovered under a rock, blinking and confused.

"You see," said Rupert O'Brien. "The late Mr Newton has been vindicated once again."

Fatty arose painfully to his feet, muttered his thanks, and holding the inadequate towel round his waist, picked his way, barefoot over the rough cobbles, back into the building.

"What a scream!" said Rupert O'Brien to Niamh, when she reappeared in the courtyard. "Have you ever seen anything so perfectly comic? French farce, my dear. Utter French farce, and all laid on for us absolutely free!

It's *Les Fouberies de Scapin* and *Le Bourgeois Gentilhomme* all rolled into one! Priceless!"

8

AFTER WATCHING HER HUSBAND BEING carried out of the room in the bath, uncertain as to whether she should accompany him (as a widow might accompany a cortège) but deciding not to do so, Betty returned to her bed. She felt profoundly discouraged by the morning's events and wondered whether the idea of coming to Ireland had been a mistake. Her visions of quiet days spent enjoying the delights of the Irish countryside and the Irish table seemed to have been a hopelessly romantic misconception. The reality of Ireland was proving quite different; gravity, so cruel and unforgiving at home in Arkansas, seemed every bit as unremitting here, where it had subjected her husband to tribulations as onerous as any that had beset him on the other, correct side of the Atlantic. What was the point, she wondered, of travelling such distances only to find that the world revealed an identically unkind face? Perhaps it would have been better to remain in America, where at least the odds seemed less stacked against generously-built people.

She decided that when Fatty returned she would ask him whether he wanted to persist with the holiday. It would involve no loss of face, she would tell him, to change their reservations and fly home that very evening. Nobody at home need know that they had returned prematurely, as they could quietly slip off for a few days somewhere and nobody would be any the wiser.

By the time that the freshly released Fatty returned to the bedroom, Betty had dozed off, her head full of reassuring thoughts of home. She opened her eyes with a start to find Fatty, clad in his towel, searching the room for his clothes.

"I'm back," he declared simply.

She rose from her bed and embraced him.

"It must have been so uncomfortable," said Betty, pushing a stray lock of hair off Fatty's brow. "I've been thinking that perhaps we should go home ... Ireland seems to be so ... " She searched for the expression. What precisely was wrong with Ireland? The food? Well, she was in no position to pass judgement on that, as they had not had the opportunity to sample any Irish dishes yet. Since they had arrived at Shannon, they had, in fact, had no more than a little soup and a few pieces of bread at dinner. She had certainly *seen* some food that morning, when she had observed Rupert O'Brien eating kedgeree with such obvious enjoyment, but that alone gave her no grounds to pronounce on the national cuisine.

Was it general discomfort then? Again, this was a charge for which she had no evidence: Mountpenny House seemed comfortable enough, even if the bathroom now lacked a bath. (They could hardly complain about that.) No. The main objection to Ireland was its *Irishness*, or rather its *wrong sort of Irishness*. Everybody at home knew what it was to be Irish, and behaved accordingly, with St Patrick's Day parades and sentimental dinners. But did the Irish themselves know how to be Irish? She was less confident of that.

"Do you want to go home?" she blurted out. "Home to Fayetteville, I mean."

Fatty looked at her uncomprehendingly.

"But of course we'll go home," he said. "We're booked to go home at the end of next week."

"But are you enjoying yourself?" she persisted.

"Am I enjoying myself in Ireland?" he asked. "Of course I am! Who couldn't enjoy himself in Ireland?"

Betty struggled to conceal her surprise. "But all these things that have been happening," she said. "Don't you feel ...."

She did not finish. "They've been nothing," said Fatty. "A few minor irritations. You know that I'm not that easily discouraged, Betty. You should know that by now."

Betty swallowed. She would have to put a brave face on it and carry on, since that was so clearly what Fatty wished to do. And it would be possible – just – to be positive: they would have a good breakfast, and that would surely raise the spirits. Then perhaps they would take a walk, or perhaps drive in the car to one of the nearby villages. The run of bad luck – for that is what it seemed to be – would have to come to an end sometime, as it could hardly go on forever and it was difficult to see what further humiliations Ireland could be planning for Fatty.

They dressed, Fatty donning the trousers which had been let out for him by Mr Delaney and one of the adapted shirts, while Betty wore the green linen trouser suit she had bought for the trip. Then they made their way down to the dining room, the door of which had been wedged closed and had to be pushed open by Fatty.

"I'm absolutely starving," said Fatty as they entered the room. "I haven't really eaten properly for over twenty-four hours!"

The thought of the impending meal made it possible to contemplate with equanimity the chance of finding Rupert O'Brien in the dining room. But Fatty need not have worried. Not only was Rupert O'Brien not there, but there was nobody else either. In fact, the dining room was completely deserted and the tables cleared.

Fatty stood at the doorway and looked at his watch.

"It's only ten," he said, his voice weak and dispirited. "Do you think that they've stopped serving already?"

Betty, who had spotted a bell, strode over to ring it. Shortly thereafter the young girl from the village, who had served the diners the previous evening, appeared from the kitchen, a dishcloth draped over her arm. She looked surprised.

"Well," she said. "Who rang the bell then? What's the emergency?"

"We were hoping for breakfast," said Fatty. "Some kedgeree perhaps?"

The waitress shook her head. "Mr O'Brien finished the kedgeree," she said. "And anyway, it's far too late for breakfast. The kitchen's closed."

Fatty exchanged an anguished glance with Betty. "But we had no dinner," he complained. "And now you're telling us that we're to get no breakfast."

The girl looked sympathetic. "That's an awful shame," she said. "But I can't re-open the kitchen once chef has closed it. He gets into an awful temper if he sees me cooking when I'm meant to be cleaning everything up. I really can't help you there."

Fatty looked miserably at the waitress.

"What time will lunch be served?" he asked.

"We don't serve lunch today," she said. "But I do have some sandwiches made up. They were going to be for Mr and Mrs O'Brien, but they haven't come to collect them yet although I told them they should fetch them by nine. I can give them to you and tell the O'Briens they were too late. I don't much take to that Jacko, if the truth be told."

Fatty was delighted, and readily accepted the offer in spite of Betty's evident reluctance to deprive the O'Briens of their lunch.

"Is it quite right, Fatty?" she asked hesitantly. "If the sandwiches were originally meant for Mr and Mrs O'Brien, then would the Lord want us to eat them?"

Fatty brushed aside her objection. "Is it right?" he exploded. "Is it right that we should get a tiny bit of the food that that fellow is trying to reserve all for himself? Of course it's right. Look at how much he's eaten since he arrived. All that dinner – when we had none, none at all – and then all the kedgeree this morning. And did he leave us so much as a scrap? He did not!"

The waitress, who had slipped off into the kitchen, now returned with a large packet of sandwiches, which she thrust into Fatty's hands.

"Don't let them be seeing it now," she whispered. "Three chicken sandwiches and three smoked salmon."

"Just the ticket!" said Fatty.

They thanked their benefactress and retired to the drawing room to eat the sandwiches.

"She's a good girl, that girl in the kitchen," Fatty said as he bit into the first of the smoked-salmon sandwiches. "She's got that O'Brien fellow's number all right."

There was a noise behind them, and Fatty swung round to see Rupert and Niamh O"Brien standing in the doorway.

"Did I hear my name being mentioned?" said the critic.

Fatty glanced away. His mouth was full of smoked-salmon sandwich anyway and he would have found it difficult to speak. Betty came to the rescue. "My husband was wondering where you were," she said.

"Well, here we are," said Rupert O'Brien, coming into the room. He stopped, his gaze moving to the packet of sandwiches.

"Sandwiches," said Niamh. "You see them, Rupert?"

Rupert nodded and turned to face Fatty. 'Where did you get those sandwiches, Mr O'Leary?"

Fatty tried to look indignant. "They're mine," he said.

"We asked …"

Rupert O'Brien did not let him finish. "You see, I asked for a pack of sandwiches to be made up for us. I asked yesterday evening. And when we went to the kitchen, they said there were no sandwiches."

"None at all," interjected Niamh.

"And yet here we see the two of you," continued Rupert O'Brien, "making short work of a *mountain* of sandwiches."

As he spoke, Rupert was glaring at Fatty. Now he moved forward swiftly and snatched one of the sandwiches.

"That's ours," shouted Fatty.

"Just as I thought," said Rupert. "Smoked salmon. The very thing we ordered." He stuffed the sandwich into his mouth and then, signalling to Niamh to follow him, left the room.

"How dare he!" muttered Fatty, once they had gone. "How dare he come in here and eat one of our sandwiches."

"Well, they were his," said Betty mildly.

Fatty snorted dismissively. "Let's finish them, Betty, before any other passer-by comes and eats them."

Within a rather short time there were only crumbs left. Fatty looked out of the window. The surface of the lough was a pale blue, reflecting the clear morning sky above.

In the distance, at the edge of the lawn, was the jetty and beyond it the boathouse. His hunger assuaged, Fatty had an idea.

"We shall go fishing," he announced. "That is what we'll do this morning, Betty."

Mrs O'Connor had invited them to use the rowing boat that they had spotted tied up at the jetty, and had pointed out a small room where the fishing tackle was stored.

"You could have a grand day on the lough," she had said. "And if you catch a nice big pike I can get chef to serve it to everybody tonight! Mind you catch a fish now!"

It took them half a hour or so to prepare the fishing rods and the lures, but at last they were standing on the jetty, with the sky above them a promising blue and the surface of the lough stretching out glass-smooth into the distance.

Fatty stood with his hands clasped behind him and drew in a deep breath.

"This is perfect, Betty," he said. "You must admit that everything is beginning to turn out well after all. I knew that things would get better."

Betty smiled. It gave her pleasure to see Fatty so happy, and she was looking forward to a few relaxing hours on the lough. She was not particularly keen on fishing, but she viewed it as the only predominantly masculine pursuit which kept men occupied and *under control* for hours on end. When he was fishing, a man could hardly be getting up to any mischief, as men tended to do if left to their own devices – standing about in the water, casting metal hooks into the depths, was, in every respect, an innocent pursuit.

They loaded the fishing gear into the boat and then, after Betty had lowered herself on to a seat in the stern, Fatty untied the painter and stepped on to the middle seat, alongside the oars and rowlocks. With a deft push at the side of the jetty, he sent the boat out into the lough and began to row, dipping the oars expertly into the water.

It was not a large boat and the combined weight of Fatty and Betty made it ride dangerously low in the water. In fact, when Betty put her hand on the side, her fingers dipped into the lough.

"This is rather low," she ventured. "If I put my hands …"

"What?" said Fatty, who was exerting himself with the rowing.

"Rather low in the water," warned Betty. "I don't know if it's going to be terribly easy to fish. All that movement."

"We'll be fine," said Fatty. "Don't you worry."

Betty was not sure, but Fatty, who was experienced with

boats, had reassured her and she decided to concentrate on enjoying the outing rather than worrying. Fatty, having rowed them some twenty yards beyond the jetty, now decided to rest for a while, and he shipped the oars, shifting slightly in his seat as he did so. It was not a large or sudden movement, but so meagre was the clearance from the surface that it proved sufficient to tilt one side of the boat under the water. With a sudden glistening rush, like molten silver being poured into a vat, the clear water of the lough flooded into the boat.

Betty shrieked, and Fatty instinctively moved in the opposite direction. But of course the correction was too great, and this only resulted in further flooding. With the boat now half-filled with water and the sides only mere inches above the surface, Fatty gingerly rowed back towards the jetty. They almost made it, but not quite. When still a few yards off, a ripple in the surface of the water was enough to tip the scales against them, and the rowing boat began to founder, dipping below the surface of the lough like a tiny stricken liner sinking beneath the waves.

Fortunately, the water at the site of their sinking was not deep, and when they involuntarily abandoned ship both Fatty and Betty found that the water came up only as far as their necks. So even had they not been able to swim, they would have been able to walk ashore – slow progress, though, with their feet in the mud and weeds of the lough bottom.

Fatty was first to clamber on to the jetty, and, from his position of safety he bent down and gave a hand to Betty, who needed assistance in getting out of the water. Betty grasped his hand and tried to pull herself up, but Fatty, vulnerable in his waterlogged footwear, slipped and toppled over into the lough; so might a hippopotamus fall into the Limpopo, with just such a splash.

"Oh Betty!" moaned Fatty, when he broke the surface. "Oh Betty, I've gone and lost my shoes now."

Betty tried to help him find his shoes, ducking under the water to do so. But they had churned up so much mud that it was impossible to see through the turbid murk, and so they reluctantly gave up and waded towards the shore. As they staggered out of the water, brushing off the weed and slime that they had acquired on their ignominious journey, they looked up and saw two figures on the lawn of the house. These two had watched the unfolding tragedy from afar, but had been unable to help, given the rapid course of events. Now, however, they strode across the lawns to enquire of the unfortunate couple as to whether they could offer any assistance.

"My dear Mr O'Leary," said Rupert O'Brien, as he tried ineffectively to brush the aquatic detritus from Fatty's shoulders. "What fearful bad luck! Did you overload that little boat, do you think? Is that what happened?"

Fatty did not reply to Rupert O'Brien. He was chilled to the bone by his exposure to the cold waters of the lough. He had no shoes. His clothes were covered with waterweed.

He turned to Betty, who stood shivering beside him, the green linen trouser suit clinging to her every bulge.

"Come Betty," he said, with such dignity as he could muster. "We'll go and have a hot bath."

"But we don't have a bath," said Betty. "Not any more."

9

Mrs O'Connor appeared largely unconcerned about the loss of the boat, just as she had accepted, with remarkable equanimity, the removal of the bath and its apparent abandonment in the courtyard.

"That boat's gone down before now," she said, as Fatty hesitantly explained their dripping and shivering arrival in the entrance hall. "I'll send Delaney's boy down to bring it up. He's a great swimmer, that lad."

She surveyed her guests with concern. "But you poor things must be most uncomfortable, and you'll be needing a good hot bath."

Fatty wrung his hands together in an attempt to restore warmth to his frozen fingers. "Our own bath, of course, is still …"

"Of course," said Mrs O'Connor. "How silly of me. You must use my own bathroom. I'll show you where it is. There's lashings of hot water and I'll get you some fresh towels."

She led them down a corridor to the bathroom. There, although Fatty took great care to ensure that he did not again become wedged in the tub, they were soon restored to warmth. Then, wearing the bathrobes that

Mrs O'Connor had thoughtfully provided for them, they made their way back to their own room and were soon warmly clad again.

"It could have been worse," said Fatty, as he sat in front of their window and gazed out over the lough. "If the boat had capsized when we were way out in the middle then heaven knows what could have happened. We might have drowned."

"Oh don't speak like that," said Betty. "I wouldn't like to drown, Fatty. Would you?"

Fatty thought for a moment. "No," he said. "I would not like to drown, Betty," adding, "on balance."

There was silence for a moment. Then Betty spoke.

"Sometimes I dream that I lose you, Fatty," she said. "I wake up feeling so sad, as if my whole world had come to an end. Which it would, if I really did lose you."

Fatty looked at his wife. He did not deserve her, he thought. Although he had done his best as a husband, he could not believe that he merited the good fortune of having such a devoted wife. And sometimes it occurred to him that all that he seemed to bring her was awkwardness and problems. The Irish trip was an example; the chapter of accidents that had unfolded since their arrival was not Betty's doing, it was his. She had not lost her luggage; she had not become stuck in the bath; she had not suggested setting forth in that inadequate boat; everything, it seemed, had been his fault.

"Do you think I'm just accident-prone?" he asked. "There are some people like that, you know. Things just go wrong for them. They don't ask for it; it just happens that way."

Betty, who had been sitting on the edge of the bed, brushing her hair, laid down her brush and came over to Fatty's side.

"Of course not, my dear," she said. "None of this is your fault. You've just had bad luck."

Fatty looked down at his bare feet. Although he had had a spare set of clothes made up by Mr Delaney, he had only one pair of shoes and now he would have to try to borrow some from Mrs O'Connor.

"I'm just not much good at things," he said. "No wonder that O'Brien person laughs at me."

Betty put her arm about his shoulder. "He doesn't laugh at you, Fatty. You haven't heard him laugh at you, have you?"

"Not to my face," said Fatty. "But behind my back. He'll be laughing at me. He'll be laughing at all the … undignified things that have happened to me."

Betty shook her head. "That's not true, my dear. And, anyway, you're a better man than he is by a long chalk. Anybody can tell that."

Fatty was silent. Something was happening at the edge of the lough and he could not quite see what it was. Rupert O'Brien was bending down at the water's edge and seemed to be poking at the surface of the lough with a stick.

"What do you think he's doing?" asked Fatty, pointing at the distant figure.

"Heaven knows," said Betty. "But let's not worry about him. Let's go for a little drive in our car. We'll buy some shoes from Mr Delaney. Then we'll have lunch somewhere. How about that?"

The mention of lunch cheered Fatty up, and he readily agreed to Betty's suggestion. Together they made their way downstairs, Betty going ahead to consult Mrs O'Connor about shoes and Fatty treading gingerly on the bare wooden floorboards, lest he pick up a splinter.

The borrowing of shoes, it transpired, was easily accomplished.

"Guests leave the most extraordinary things behind," said Mrs O'Connor, opening a large walk-in cupboard. "Look in here."

Betty saw a cornucopia of effects: walking sticks, umbrellas, coats, books and various items of clothing, all stacked on shelves. At the bottom, neatly arrayed, were lines of shoes. Her eye alighted on a handsome pair of brogues that looked as if it was the right size for Fatty: size ten, extra broad fitting.

"That's a fine pair of shoes," said Mrs O'Connor. "I have no idea who left them. But if they fit your husband, Mrs O'Leary, then he should wear them. It's an awful pity to waste shoes like that."

Fatty, who had now negotiated his way downstairs, took the shoes from Betty, along with a pair of checked men's socks that Mrs O'Connor had retrieved from one of the shelves. The fit was perfect, and the shoes were extremely comfortable. He thanked Mrs O'Connor, and together he and Betty went out to their car and drove off down the drive.

The shoes made his spirits soar, as fine apparel and the knowledge that one is wearing it tend to do.

"I feel well-shod," he remarked to Betty, as the lush countryside rolled past them. "It's extraordinary how *empowering* a good pair of shoes can be."

Betty nodded. She had read about empowerment, which was something people seemed to talk a great deal about these days. A few months previously, at the Fayetteville Charity Fair, she had paid five dollars to enter a tent intriguingly labelled: *Feminist Fortunes – the future as it really is.* The fortune-teller, a young woman with unnerving green eyes, had said to her: "Are you empowered?" Betty had been uncertain how to answer, as she was not sure whether or not she was empowered. She had never felt *unempowered* or *disempowered,* but this did not mean that she was actually empowered.

The young woman had smiled at her. "The sisters are with you,' she had said. "They will help you to forget the man who's been holding you back."

Betty looked astonished. Was Fatty holding her back? She thought it unlikely: Fatty always encouraged her to do things and took great pleasure in her achievements.

"I don't think a man's holding me back," she had said. "Not as far as I know."

The young woman had looked at her pityingly. "They all hold us back," she said. "It's just that sometimes they're subtle about it and you don't know that it's happening."

"But my husband's a nice man," she had said. "We love to do things together. We're very happy."

The young woman had shaken her head. "There's a number on this leaflet," she said, handing her a folded

109

piece of paper. "Next time he becomes violent, call us."

But talk of empowerment seemed inappropriate in this landscape; it belonged to a world of conflict, to a society that seemed to be at war with itself, where people were pitted against one another in prickly distrust. Ireland was not like that, she thought, particularly not this part of Ireland, where strangers waved to one another and everybody seemed content with their lot.

She looked out of the window. They were passing a field, which was bordered by an unkempt hedgerow; in the field, a small flock of sheep was browsing over the uneven grass; in the distance, behind a cluster of trees, rose a green hillside. The narrow road swung round, and they were at a crossroads, at which a signpost pointed in several directions, its arms loose, its message unclear.

"Not very helpful," remarked Betty; but Fatty replied, "It doesn't matter anyway", and chose the most interesting-looking road.

For the next two hours, they travelled round the country, passing through small villages and towns, taking their time and enjoying the vistas that presented themselves at every turn. They knew, in the most general of senses, where they were; as long as they kept the lough in sight, off to the north, they were safe from disappearing into the great central plain of Ireland or slipping off the cliffs of Kerry into the Atlantic. Now that Fatty had his new shoes, there was no need to revisit Nenagh, or Mr Delaney, and so they meandered purposelessly, at one with their surroundings, empowered, in an entirely Elysian sense, by the soft landscape of Ireland.

At last, just before five o'clock, they found themselves entering Balinderry, from where they knew well the final few miles home. It had been a triumphant drive; even if they were to leave that very evening, they would be able to say to their friends back home that they had *seen* Ireland. But now, the car safely parked outside Mountpenny House, they could return to their room and have a short rest before the serving of six o'clock drinks in the large drawing room. Fatty, who had enjoyed the drive immensely, felt that he could even face Rupert O'Brien now, and cope with his overweening attitude. He would not try to compete, Fatty thought; he would let him hold forth as much as he liked and simply let it wash over him. In that way anxiety would be replaced by indifference.

They were the first down at six o'clock. The late summer sun was low in the sky but it did not reach that side of the building, which made the recently lit fire welcome.

Mrs O'Connor, who had seen them going in, popped her head round the door and took orders for drinks, which she served quickly, and in generous measure.

"We have another guest this evening," she told them. "One of our regular people. He often stays when he's over buying a horse. Lord Balnerry. A very nice man. You'll like him."

Betty caught her breath. She was not at all sure that she would know what to say to somebody called Lord Balnerry. She had, in fact, never met a count or baron, or whatever, although she had always imagined Europe to be peopled by such figures. Fatty, too, was not a little nervous: the name seemed familiar for some reason, and yet he could not quite recall where he had heard it. Had there been a mention of Lord Balnerry in the *Irish Tatler*, along with Mr Cosimo Pricolo and Mr Pears van Eck, or, indeed, with Mr Rupert O'Brien … The memory suddenly returned. It was Rupert O'Brien himself who had mentioned the peer when he was talking about antiques. He had said – had he not – that he used to help Lord Balnerry sort out his "stuff" at his "place" near Cork.

Fatty's heart sank. If Lord Balnerry were a friend of Rupert O'Brien, then his ordeal would be re-doubled. He would be faced, he imagined, with a barrage from two directions. The only thing to do, he thought, would be to leave. They could quickly make some excuse and go off and have dinner somewhere else. They had seen a hotel not far away where there was a sign proclaiming a distinguished table. They could go there and have dinner in peace, without having to listen to what would surely be a litany of distinguished names, none known to them.

As soon as Mrs O'Connor had left the room, Fatty turned to Betty.

"I think, my dear," he began, "that we should perhaps go and have dinner somewhere …"

He did not have time to finish his sentence. Had he been able to do so, Betty would undoubtedly have agreed to his plan, but before anything more could be said the door so recently closed by Mrs O'Connor was opened again and a tall, well-built man in a brown tweed suit entered the room. He was wearing no tie, but had a red bandanna tied loosely round his neck. He also wore, as Fatty and Betty both noticed immediately, a large sand-coloured moustache.

"Well, well," he said. "Drinks time already. What a relief!"

He smiled broadly at Fatty and Betty and moved across to greet then, his hand extended.

Fatty rose to his feet and shook hands. "Cornelius O'Leary," he said. "And this is my wife, Betty."

Lord Balnerry shook hands with Fatty and then gave a small bow in the direction of Betty.

"Monty Balnerry," he said.

Mrs O'Connor now returned, bearing her drinks tray.

"I've mixed the usual for you, Lord Balnerry," she said. "Very large whiskey and soda with a dash of extra whiskey for good effect."

The drinks were passed round. Fatty, who had felt a momentary sense of being trapped when his proposal had been interrupted by the arrival of the new guest, found himself immediately re-assured. Lord Balnerry was clearly going to be easy company.

"You people American?" asked Lord Balnerry.

"Yes," said Fatty. "We're from Fayetteville, Arkansas."

Lord Balnerry smiled. "Marvellous place, Arkansas. I've been there several times. I was in Fayetteville a couple of years ago. I loved it."

"You've been to Fayetteville?" Betty asked incredulously. "Are you sure?"

Lord Balnerry laughed. "I'm pretty sure I have," he said. "I stayed with my old friend Rob Leflar. Do you know him?"

"Of course we do," said Fatty, beaming with pleasure. "And his father too. A great man, the father."

"Of course," said Lord Balnerry. "Well, well, isn't that nice that we've got friends in common. So much for the oceans that divide us." He raised his glass to Fatty and Betty and took a large gulp of whiskey.

"That's better," said Lord Balnerry. "I've been looking at horses. It's dry work."

Fatty laughed. "Most work is."

"And yours, Mr O'Leary," said Lord Balnerry. "May I ask you what you do?"

"I'm an antiques dealer," said Fatty.

Lord Balnerry was impressed. "That's a very demanding business," he said. "I doubt if I'd be any good at it."

"I'm sure you would," said Fatty.

"Oh no," said Lord Balnerry. "I'm not very bright. Peers rarely are."

There was silence for a moment. Fatty and Betty were not certain how to take this, but Lord Balnerry continued breezily. "I can remember horses, of course. I cope with that. But concepts are a bit more demanding. Always have been."

Betty glanced at Fatty, hoping for guidance, but Fatty himself was perplexed.

"So," mused Lord Balnerry. "I'd be out of my depth if I had to do your job."

Fatty found himself warming more and more to their new companion. There was no pretentiousness about him – unlike Rupert O'Brien, of course – and there was a quality of friendliness which radiated out from the tweed suit and the drooping moustache like an electro-magnetic field. But just as he was reflecting on this, the door opened again, and in came Rupert and Niamh O'Brien. Niamh was wearing a long cocktail dress and Rupert O'Brien had donned a lightweight cream jacket from the breast pocket of which emanated a large, red handkerchief. As they entered, their gaze moved immediately to Lord Balnerry, who was standing with his back to the fireplace, his large glass of whiskey in one hand and the other hand tucked into his pocket.

"Lord Balnerry!' exclaimed Rupert O'Brien. "What a pleasant surprise! Our hostess told us that you might be here. How good to see you again."

"Oh," said Lord Balnerry. "Oh, yes. Of course. Of course."

Fatty looked up at the aristocrat and realised immediately that Lord Balnerry had no idea of who it was who was addressing him.

116

"This is Mr O'Brien," said Fatty confidently. "And Mrs O'Brien of course. Mr and Mrs O'Brien, from Dublin."

Rupert O'Brien cast a withering glance in Fatty's direction.

"No need to introduce us," he said. "We've known one another for a long time."

Lord Balnerry looked briefly at Fatty, who seemed crestfallen. In an instant he assessed the situation, and assessed it correctly. "Oh have we?" he said sharply to Rupert O'Brien. "Forgive me for not recalling your name, sir. In my position I meet so many *members of the public* that I find I forget them. You must forgive me. What did you say your name was again?"

Rupert O'Brien stood stock-still, as if he had received an electric shock. When he spoke, his voice sounded uncertain.

"Rupert O'Brien," he said. "You may not remember, but I have been to your house, several times."

"To do work there?" asked Lord Balnerry. "Tradesman?"

Fatty thought that he heard the sharp intake of breath from Rupert O'Brien.

"Certainly not," said O'Brien. "I'm with the *Irish Times*."

"Don't read it," said Lord Balnerry.

It was fortunate, perhaps, that Mrs O'Connor returned at this point with drinks for the O'Briens. They took their glasses in shaking hands and sat down.

"Anyway," said Lord Balnerry, "as I was saying to my friend Mr O'Leary, it's remarkable how small the world is. He and I find that we have a very good friend in common."

Rupert O'Brien appeared to rally. "Of course," he said, jovially. "And you and I have many friends in common too. Senator Cuilhain, for example. He and I are very close."

"He's a shocker," said Lord Balnerry. "I wouldn't get too close to him if I were you. He's no friend of mine. Sorry."

Rupert O'Brien decided to treat this remark as a joke. "Oh, very droll," he said. "A shocker! Poor old Paddy Cuilhain."

"I wasn't joking," said Lord Balnerry. "I meant it, Mr O'Sullivan."

"O'Brien," corrected Rupert O'Brien.

"Another shocker," said Lord Balnerry.

The conversation drifted, with Rupert O'Brien trying, quite unsuccessfully, to turn it to his advantage. At last, on the verge of despair, he turned to Fatty and said: "I retrieved your shoes from the lough, Mr O'Leary. They floated, and I fished them out with a stick. They're drying outside."

Everybody looked at Fatty's feet.

"But I see that you brought another pair with you," went on O'Brien. "That was wise."

Fatty noticed that Lord Balnerry was staring at his new brogues. "Funny," said Lord Balnerry. "I had a pair just like that, but I left them somewhere …"

Fatty's heart thumped wildly within him. He must, at all costs, divert attention from his shoes. But how to do it?

Rupert O'Brien chipped in. "I have a wonderful shoemaker in Dublin. He takes a last of your feet and then keeps it forever. He made a pair for my father and I'm still wearing them. Wonderful shoes. Can you wear your father's shoes, Lord Balnerry?"

Lord Balnerry's gaze moved from Fatty's shoes.

"He only had one leg," he said curtly. "Therefore he only had one shoe."

Rupert O'Brien blushed. "I'm so sorry," he said.

They went through for dinner, Lord Balnerry taking Betty's arm and courteously accompanying her, while Fatty walked on his other side. Rupert and Niamh O'Brien followed, both with angry, furrowed brows. The smoking jacket, so elegant on first appearance, now seemed a less secure fit, and Niamh's bearing, previously haughty and remote, was marginally less self-assured.

Lord Balnerry took it upon himself to arrange the seating at the table. Betty was invited to sit on his right, and Fatty on his left. The O'Briens were left to take the remaining seats. Once seated, though, Rupert O'Brien seemed determined to make up lost ground. Taking the menu, he scrutinised it carefully. "Let's see what Mrs O'Connor is tempting us with," he said. "Ah! I see we are to start with gravlax with mustard sauce. That's delightful. We had that, did we not, my dear, at Antoine's in Dublin the other day. You know the place, Lord Balnerry?"

"Yes," said Lord Balnerry. "I know it."

"Wonderful chef, Antoine," said Rupert O'Brien, now getting into his stride. "We often have a little chat with him afterwards. He sometimes even tells Niamh his recipes, which these great chefs can't stand doing, you know. They regard them as a trade secret. That's why you must never ask a chef for his recipe. It's a terrible thing to do."

"Oh, but I do," said Lord Balnerry. "I always ask."

"Ah!" said Rupert O'Brien. "I'm sure you know when you can ask. I didn't say that you should *never* ask. I just said that you shouldn't. You'll know when you can."

"But I always ask," said Lord Balnerry. "All the time."

"Ha!" said Rupert O'Brien. "Well, there you are. No matter. Antoine doesn't like it, but he always gives Niamh a tip about some dish or other. He used to cook for Freddy Guinness before he started his own restaurant. You know Freddy Guinness?"

"My cousin," said Lord Balnerry. Then, turning to Betty, he said: "You have a very good restaurant in Fayetteville. My friends took me there. Everything is so pleasant in Arkansas."

"Thank you," said Betty, beaming with pleasure.

"You been to Arkansas, Mr O'Brien?" asked Lord Balnerry.

"No," said Rupert O'Brien. "But …"

"Pity," said Lord Balnerry. "It's a charming state. You should go there."

"Well," said Rupert O'Brien. "I'm often in New York, you know."

Lord Balnerry reached for his glass of water. "Never go there myself."

The meal progressed. The waitress, who was the same waitress who had given Fatty and Betty the sandwiches she had made for the O'Briens, seemed very fond of Lord Balnerry and responded well to his suggestion that she give generous helpings to their "American friends" so that they should return home with a positive impression of Irish hospitality. It was a concomitant of this, of course, that there was less for the O'Briens, whose plates arrived barely covered, while Fatty and Betty received large mounds of delicious food. And then, entirely accidentally, at the end of the meal she spilt the remnants of a raspberry sorbet over Rupert O'Brien's white jacket, for which accident she apologised profusely, but was defended stoutly by Lord Balnerry.

"Don't worry," he said quickly. "Mr O'Brien understands how hard it must be to be a waitress and not spill things. I'm always spilling things myself. I spilled soup over Freddy Guinness once. You won't know him, O'Brien, but he's a very charming man, and he didn't make me feel bad about it, not for one second."

Over coffee, Rupert O'Brien and Niamh sat in silence. Lord Balnerry continued his easy conversation with Fatty and Betty and, just before he looked at his watch and announced that it was time to retire to bed, he issued his invitation.

"You must come and spend a weekend with me, Cornelius and Betty," he said genially. "I have a place near Cork. It would be grand to have you over for a weekend, or even a week if you can spare the time. Please do make a point of it. But anyway, I'll see you tomorrow, as we arranged."

Fatty and Betty immediately replied that they would love to do this. And then there was a silence. Rupert O'Brien was sitting on the edge of his seat, but nothing more was said. There was no further invitation and Lord Balnerry now rose to his feet and bade goodnight to the assembled company.

"What a charming man," said Fatty, after Lord Balnerry had left the room.

"Yes," said Betty. "He was so warm and kind to us. He made us feel so special. What a nice, nice man. And a lord too."

Rupert O'Brien looked steadfastly at the ceiling.

"Well, good night," said Fatty, rising to his feet. "We've had a busy day and we have a lot to do tomorrow. Lord Balnerry invited us to accompany him to the horse sales tomorrow. Will you be coming too?"

"No," said Rupert O'Brien.

In their room, they lay together holding hands across the space between their beds.

"He was such a kind man," said Betty. "I really felt as if

I had known him for years."

"That's what people here are really like," said Fatty. "We should have realised it. After all, think of all the kindness we've met since we came here. That kind Mr Delaney and then Mrs O'Connor, and even the plumber. And now Lord Balnerry himself."

"He made me feel so clever," said Betty. "He seemed so interested in everything I said."

"But you are clever, my dear," said Fatty. "And everything you say really is interesting."

They lapsed into comfortable, companionable silence. Outside, in the Irish night, an owl swooped across Mrs O'Connor's lawns, and then disappeared into the woods.

10

Lord Balnerry, who had driven up from Cork in his horsebox, thought there was no point in Fatty and Betty driving their car to the sales when there was ample room in his vehicle.

'I've got three seats in the front," he said. 'And there are three of us. No sense in your trailing behind me. We'll all go together."

Mrs O'Connor personally prepared packed lunches for them: duck sandwiches, three generous slices of Melton Mowbray pie and half a fruitcake lightly soaked in rum. Then, their cameras loaded to record the day's experiences, Fatty and Betty joined Lord Balnerry beside the horsebox. It was a large, grey-painted vehicle, with a narrow, wood-slatted section at the rear where a horse might stand in passable comfort. On the engine grille were lined the insignia of various motoring clubs, gleaming silver badges with crests and symbols, survivors of an easier age of motoring.

Lord Balnerry opened the passenger door and invited Betty to get in. She squeezed herself into the narrow confines of the cab, realising immediately that the seats were far too small for a further passenger, even one of modest girth.

"I'm not sure if we're all going to fit," she said, trying to slide further over the seat towards the middle. "It's rather cramped in here."

Lord Balnerry stepped forward and looked through the open passenger door.

"I see what you mean," he said. "I'm used to carrying jockeys in there. I've had four people in before this, but then you know what jockeys are like. Tiny fellows. You're not exactly ..." He stopped, and turned to Fatty.

"Would you mind terribly, Cornelius?" he said. "I often let my nephew travel in the horse's quarters. It's perfectly comfortable back there."

Fatty hesitated for a moment. It was preposterous to ask somebody to travel in a horse's stall, with all the straw and the smell. Did Lord Balnerry think that he was not worth more than that? Would he have asked another lord to do that? What about Freddy Guinness? Would he have asked Freddy Guinness to subject himself to that? Or was it just because he was merely Fatty O'Leary from Fayetteville, Arkansas that he thought he could make the suggestion?

Fatty stared at Lord Balnerry, looking for a clue in his expression; perhaps a curl of the lip or an incipient sneer. But there was nothing. Lord Balnerry seemed utterly sincere.

"I'd travel in it myself," he said, "and let you drive. But this thing is only insured for me and you know how careful we have to be in Ireland now that we've got Brussels breathing down our necks. In the old days nobody bothered about insurance or anything like that. But these days, it's a different story. The Belgians can send you to prison for all sorts of things these days. Even for thinking the wrong sort of thoughts, I should imagine."

Fatty smiled. "I don't mind," he said. "I can look out through the slats and see what's going on. I'll be fine."

"Good man," said Lord Balnerry, beginning to undo the back gate of the box. "Here we are now. Lots of hay if you get hungry!"

Fatty laughed as he walked up the ramp, but stopped when, from the corner of his eye, he spotted a figure standing at the back door of the house, watching proceedings with a keen interest. Although he turned away quickly and scampered up the last of the ramp, he knew that it had been Rupert O'Brien.

"Would you believe it," said Rupert O'Brien to Niamh, when he returned to the drawing room. "I've just seen that forgetful Monty Balnerry loading our well-padded American friend into the back of his horse box – just like a horse! Madly comic, my dear! We have no need of further entertainment out here, believe me. These rustic types are just too screamingly funny for words. I've got a good mind to write it up in my next column. *The adventures of a Substantial Man in Ireland, Part One.* The embarrassments to which the flesh is heir. Hah! What about that?"

Niamh tossed aside the magazine she had been reading.

"Nobody would believe it, my dear," Niamh drawled. "But I'm glad that you're being entertained like this. I find the whole place too excruciatingly boring. I could commit murder for a bit of decent company, not that I'm bored with you, my dear, perish the thought. You're fine, in your way, but you know how it is?"

"Of course I do," said Rupert, urbanely. "One's spouse's face is always so, how should one put it? – familiar. Just like a pair of old slippers. Not referring to you, my dear, of course. Hah!"

Lord Balnerry closed the doors behind Fatty.

"Hope it's not too dark, Cornelius," he called out. "You'll get a bit of light through the chinks. Horses usually prefer to travel in the dark. They get less nervous that way."

Fatty grunted. The straw was quite clean, and he had sat down upon it, resting against the side of the box. It would be comfortable enough, he supposed, even if it was rather less than dignified. It was not a long journey to the sales – fifteen or twenty minutes, Lord Balnerry had told him – and he could easily put up with this unconventional method of travelling for that length of time. If only that Rupert O'Brien had not seen him. What would he make of it? He would have some snide remark to pass, no doubt.

In the cabin in the front, Betty and Lord Balnerry chatted easily as they drove along the narrow winding lanes.

"I've got a feeling that there are going to be some good horses for sale today," Lord Balnerry said. "There are one or two I'm strongly interested in. Good runners. Best horses in Ireland, some of them. I'd be very happy to give them a home."

Betty smiled. She understood enthusiasm for horses, as one of her brothers had married the daughter of a Kentucky stud farmer and had become completely smitten with the pursuit. She knew nothing about horses, of course, but when it came to chickens and to hogs she knew a great deal. People took chickens for granted and could not understand breeding lines, but she knew better. There were chicken lines in Arkansas which were every bit as distinguished as horse lines in Kentucky – less pricey, perhaps, but as important in their own way.

After little more than a quarter of an hour they reached the edge of the town where the horse sales were to be held. A field had been taken over for the purpose and a large white marquee had been erected in the centre. All about the periphery of the field horse boxes very similar to theirs had been parked, and it was at the end of a line of these that Lord Balnerry drew the vehicle to a halt and went to open the doors at the back.

Fatty O'Leary was dead. Or so it seemed to Lord Balnerry, who gave a shout of alarm when he pulled on the spring-loaded door and saw the figure of his friend sprawled out on the straw.

"Oh my God!" said Lord Balnerry. "The poor fellow."

The flood of light and the sound of Lord Balnerry's voice woke Fatty immediately. Sitting up in the straw, he rubbed his eyes and looked out on to the field full of horses and people.

"Thank heavens!" said Lord Balnerry. "You gave me a terrible fright there!"

"I was tired," said Fatty, as he rose to his feet and dusted down his trousers. "That straw was as comfortable as any bed. I had a nice little nap, I believe, and here we are at the horse sales already."

Lord Balnerry helped his guest down the ramp and

then, joined by Betty, they made their way over to the marquee, which served as both office and bar. Lord Balnerry seemed to be known to most of the people present, as he was greeted warmly on every side.

"Amongst friends," he whispered to Fatty. "Frightfully good occasion, this. Best sort of people in Ireland are here. Horse people. Can't beat them. Salt of the earth."

Fatty looked about him at the tweed suits and the heavy shoes, at the ruddy faces and the caps and walking sticks and other signs of good, country blood. They were very different types from antiques people, but he understood exactly what Lord Balnerry meant. These people were the opposite of Rupert and Niamh O'Brien, with all their talk of literature and their name-dropping. These people were honest.

They spent a short time in the tent, during which Fatty and Betty were introduced to a number of Lord Balnerry's friends. Then a hand bell was rung at the other end of the field and they drifted over to an area that had been partitioned off and around which racked seating had been erected. This was the show-ring into which the horses would be led for sale.

Fatty and Betty joined Lord Balnerry on one of the benches near the front and waited for the first horse to be brought into the ring. They had been given a programme for the sale, and they saw that this horse, a slightly nervous bay gelding, had been bred by Mr Harry McDermott of Finaghy Stud, near Tralee. It had been sired by Round Robin out of Kerry Autumn, and was two years old.

"Dreadful horse," whispered Lord Balnerry. "Round Robin was well-named, if you ask me. Great tub of lard of a horse. Barely get himself over the jumps. Terrible lazy fellow. The only reason I'd buy this horse would be to sell him to the French and let them turn him into a pie."

Fatty looked at the unfortunate horse; he could not see why Lord Balnerry should be so scathing about him, and he noticed that the bidding had started quite briskly.

"Fools," whispered Lord Balnerry, as he heard the bids mount up. "That fellow will get nowhere. Fools."

The horse sold well, as did the following two horses. In each case Lord Balnerry shook his head sorrowfully at the apparent lack of judgement of his fellow Irishmen.

"This would never happen in Kentucky, would it Cornelius?" he said. "Those horses would be laughed out of the sales rings. I know. I've been there."

These comments were unfortunately overheard by one of the purchasers sitting further along the bench. He turned round and glared angrily at Lord Balnerry, who smiled and nodded in a placatory way. He was about to say something, when his attention was caught by the entry of the next horse into the ring. He stared hard at it and tapped Fatty on the arm.

"Now there's a horse," he said. "Would you look at that fellow, Cornelius. Would you look at that way he carries his head. That's not only a good horse, that's a great horse."

Fatty and Betty gazed at the horse. It was certainly livelier than the previous ones and its coat shone with health.

"That's a beauty," said Betty. "That's going to be a winner."

"Exactly," said Lord Balnerry. "Never a truer word spoken by an American lady. With a horse like that one could win Ascot. One would romp home against all those fancy French horses at Deauville. And would you look at its name: *Ireland's Hope*. What a find!"

"Are you going to bid for it?" asked Fatty.

"I am that," said Lord Balnerry. "I don't know how long I'll be able to stay in the bidding, but I'm going to have a stab at it. I could go places with that horse."

The bidding opened at five thousand pounds. Lord Balnerry waited for a short while the initial bids were made but then joined in when the field had narrowed to a man and a woman at the far side of the ring.

"Ten thousand to Lord Balnerry," called out the auctioneer. "For this fine horse. Any advance on Lord Balnerry's bid of ten thousand?"

The man on the far side of the ring raised his hand and an extra thousand pounds was added to the bid.

Fatty turned to Lord Balnerry, who had now shaken his head.

"Are you going to bid?" he asked.

"Past my limit," whispered Lord Balnerry. "That's me out."

"Eleven thousand to Mr O'Malley over here," said the auctioneer. "Eleven thousand for this fine young horse with all his future ahead of him. Any advance on eleven thousand pounds?"

Fatty was suddenly aware of Lord Balnerry's hand on his elbow.

"My goodness," said Lord Balnerry. "Isn't that Mrs O'Connor over there waving to you? Give her a wave, Cornelius."

Fatty looked across the ring and saw Mrs O'Connor standing near the entrance to the ring. Instinctively he raised his hand and waved.

"Twelve thousand," said the auctioneer. "Twelve thousand over there. Do you want to reply, Mr O'Malley?"

O'Malley shook his head and the auctioneer raised his hammer and hit his desk, causing the horse to start skittishly.

"Sold at twelve thousand to the gentleman sitting next to Lord Balnerry. Your name, sir?"

Fatty, whose attention had been focused on Mrs O'Connor, now swung his head round and saw the auctioneer pointing directly at him.

"Your name, sir?" repeated the auctioneer.

Confused, Fatty called out: "Cornelius O'Leary."

"Thank you, sir," said the auctioneer. "Now, ladies and gentlemen, the next horse is a very interesting little filly from Fermanagh of all places. A long way from home, but a very fine prospect for next year's flat season ..."

"Oh dear me," said Lord Balnerry. "I'm afraid you bought that horse, Cornelius. He must have thought you were bidding when you waved to Mrs O'Connor over there. What a terrible mix-up."

Fatty felt the blood drain from his face. He turned to Betty, whose expression was one of mute alarm.

"I'll have to tell them," he said. "They'll have to sell it again."

"Oh they'll never do that," said Lord Balnerry. "It's strictly against the rules at these sales. Buy a horse, you've got a horse. That's the exact wording of the rules of sale, I believe." He paused, and patted Fatty on the forearm. "Still, you've got a wonderful horse. A beautiful horse, in fact."

"But I don't want a horse," said Fatty. "This is Ireland. It's an Irish horse. I live in America. What would I do with a horse over here?"

"You could take him back with you," said Lord Balnerry. "You could sell him over there. Your racing people like Irish horses. Expensive, mind you. They have to have a veterinary surgeon on the flight. Costs about five thousand to send a horse over."

Fatty let out a moan; a sound that seemed to be half way between a sigh and a cry of despair.

"I don't want it," he said. "I just don't want a horse."

Lord Balnerry now gripped his arm firmly and pulled him to his feet.

"I've got a idea," he said. I'll buy the horse from you. That means that I get the horse and you don't, which is probably what we wanted in the first place. How about that?"

Fatty felt the despair lift from his shoulders. Of course,

that was the solution. He would sell the horse to Lord Balnerry on the spot: what a neat solution to what had seemed a nightmarish situation.

"That's a fine idea," he said. "In fact, the simplest thing is for you just to go and pay. Then no money changes hands. Simple."

Lord Balnerry coughed politely.

"Well, not quite that simple, I'm afraid," he said. "Fact is, I don't have twelve thousand at hand. Most I can manage is about five. If you wouldn't mind taking five now, and then I can note you down for a share of future winnings. In a year or two we'll get the seven back to you. Who knows?"

He smiled at Fatty, and reached into his jacket pocket to extract a battered cheque book.

"Here," he said, scribbling in the cheque book. "You put the horse on your American Express card and I'll give you this cheque for five thousand. Bank of Ireland. Safe as houses. Here you are."

Fatty took the cheque in trembling hands and tucked it into his pocket.

"I don't want to stay for the rest of the sale," he said quietly. "Do you mind if we go now?"

"Of course not," said Lord Balnerry. "We'll pay, pick

up the horse, and get back to the hotel."

In the tent, the auctioneer's assistant took Fatty's card and gave him a receipt for twelve thousand pounds. Then, with a stable boy leading *Ireland's Hope*, they made their way back to the van. The horse was put inside and the door closed.

"Well," said Lord Balnerry. "That's that, then." He paused. "Oh dear, the horse is in your place, Cornelius, and there are only two seats in the cab. What are we going to do?"

"I can sit on his lap," said Betty. "I'm not leaving my husband here."

"Of course we wouldn't leave him," said Lord Balnerry. "I wasn't thinking of that. Are you sure that you'll be comfortable?"

"We've done it before," said Betty. "I used to sit on Fatty's lap when we were courting."

"Ah, the romance of youth," said Lord Balnerry cheerfully. "Well, off we go."

They drove back slowly, so as not to frighten *Ireland's Hope*. Speed would have been undesirable for other reasons: Betty was pressed hard up against the windscreen and every bump pressed her against the glass and then back against Fatty. On the final approach to Mountpenny

House, the van hit a pothole in the ground that Lord Balnerry did not spot in time, and Betty shot up towards the roof and fell heavily back against her husband.

"Oh!" shouted Fatty. "My ribs! Oh!"

When they alighted outside the house, Fatty felt a sharp pain in his side. It was severe enough to make him stop in his tracks and clutch at his chest.

"Fatty!" exclaimed Betty. "Are you all right, my dear?"

"I feel as if I have a broken rib," moaned Fatty. "There's a terrible pain right there. Oh my goodness, it's sore."

They went inside and Fatty lay down on his bed. Betty gave him a painkiller that she had obtained from the housekeeper and then waited at his bedside for the arrival of the doctor.

"It's a cracked rib, most likely," said the doctor, after he had completed his examination. "Very common sort of fracture, and not one we can do much about. I suggest that you just rest for a few days and let it get better. I'd say that you were in a nice peaceful place out here."

He looked at Fatty for confirmation, but Fatty was silent.

After the doctor had gone, and Fatty and Betty were alone together, Fatty looked up at Betty.

"I want to go home, my dear," he said. "Please take

me home, Betty. Please take me home to America. I'm a dollars and cents man. I want to go home."

"You shall, Fatty," said Betty soothingly. "Ireland hasn't been very kind to you, has it?"

Fatty closed his eyes, and then opened them again to let a tear trickle down his cheek.

LAST COURSE
A Fortunate Man

II

As Fatty sat on his porch, his feet up on his favourite stool, the branches of the oak tree planted by his grandfather scraping in their familiar way against the shingle of his roof, he reflected on how although travel may broaden the mind it also made one sharply aware of the charms of home. The wider world was a large and exciting place, but ultimately there was nowhere to match Fayetteville, Arkansas. The trip to Ireland had satisfied his curiosity, but it had convinced him that the badges of identity so glibly bandied about were exactly that: glib. He had been taught to describe himself as Irish, but he was not really Irish, or he was only Irish in the most attenuated sense. Ireland had offered him nothing but hurt and embarrassment, from the humiliations of the flight and the loss of his luggage to the final, painful ride in Lord Balnerry's horsebox. Even Lord Balnerry, charming though he undoubtedly was, seemed to have profited at Fatty's expense. Fatty had ended up buying him half a horse – for that is what it amounted to – and he could not help wondering whether this had not been engineered from the beginning. Why was Mrs O'Connor at the sales, and why did she stand on the other side of the ring and wave to him at exactly the crucial moment in the bidding? He had considered the possibility that Lord Balnerry and Mrs O'Connor were in league, and that her presence at the sales had been orchestrated by Lord Balnerry. But if that was the case, then he had been taken advantage of by the very man whom he thought had treated him so courteously in the face of the onslaught from that awful Rupert O'Brien. But perhaps even that was part of the larger plot. It could be that Rupert O'Brien and Lord Balnerry were in fact close friends and that Lord Balnerry was only pretending to snub him in order to win Fatty's trust. That was an awful possibility, and the mere thought of it made Fatty depressed.

But whatever conclusion he reached, he was determined to keep it private. Betty may eventually have realised that he was unhappy, and indeed it was Betty who arranged for their early return home, but even with Betty he was determined to put a positive construction on the whole matter and to say that the trip, although disappointing in some respects, had been, on the whole, a success. Certainly this was the approach he took with his friends Tubby O'Rourke and Porky Flanagan. They and their wives called on Fatty and Betty for dinner a few days after their return and were shown photographs of

Mountpenny House and the surrounding villages.

"We must go there too," said Porky Flanagan. "Perhaps all Irish people should go to Ireland at least once. Like Muslims to Mecca or …"

"Hindus to the …" suggested Tubby. "Hindus to the river."

Porky stared at the photograph of Mountpenny House that Fatty had taken from the entrance to the walled vegetable garden.

"Who's that?" he asked, pointing to a figure standing in the doorway of the main house.

Fatty looked at the photograph. He had not studied it closely before, and now that he did so he saw the unmistakeable figure of Rupert O'Brien, smiling at the camera from a distance. The photograph was ruined, of course, and would have to be thrown away; but that could come later.

"One of the other guests," said Fatty. "A man called O'Brien. A literary critic, I believe."

"My!" said Hibernia Flanagan. "You sure moved in smart circles over there."

Fatty did not reply. He took the photograph from Porky and slid it under the bottom of the pile.

"Now this one here," he said, extracting a photograph

of Lord Balnerry that he took at the horse sales (before the disaster). "This one here is our friend, Lord Balnerry. We went to the horse sales together, didn't we Betty?"

"We sure did," said Betty.

"Did you buy a horse then?" laughed Tubby O'Rourke.

There was a moment's silence. Fatty glanced at Betty, but she had just risen to her feet to attend to something in the kitchen and she did not catch his glance. He looked down at his feet.

Tubby looked puzzled. "Did I say something?"

"Yes," said Porky. "You asked Fatty if he bought a horse. A damn stupid question, if you ask me. Why would Fatty buy a horse? You wouldn't buy a horse, would you, Fatty?"

Fatty opened his mouth to speak, but was interrupted by Tubby.

"I didn't mean it seriously," he interjected. "I know that Fatty wouldn't be so stupid as to buy a horse. You wouldn't buy a horse, would you, Fatty?"

Fatty swallowed. "Why would I buy a horse in Ireland?" He laughed, adding, insouciantly: "Why would I buy a horse anywhere?"

"I don't know," said Tubby. "People buy horses for all sorts of reasons. You never know."

"But that's not the point," persisted Porky. "The question is not why people in general buy horses, but why Fatty would have a reason to buy a horse. You wouldn't buy a horse, would you, Fatty?"

Fatty looked at Porky. His friend's expression was earnest, and showed confidence in his good judgement, but he wished that Porky would let the matter drop.

"Well," he said, chuckling, "I don't know about you, but horses don't mean very much to me. Not that I'm against them or anything like that. It's just that horses don't interest me."

"Well, why go to a horse sale, then?" asked Tubby. "It seems a bit odd to me."

Fatty sighed, as if explaining a simple situation to one whose grasp of it was dubious.

"The reason why I went to the horse sale," he said, "was because Lord Balnerry – this man in the photograph – who was a lord we met in Ireland, well, he asked us to the sale. He wanted to buy a horse. Betty and I went because we wanted to see what happened at an Irish horse sale. That's why."

Betty now entered the room, carrying a plate of sandwiches.

"Did Fatty tell you about his horse?" she asked brightly.

Again the room became silent. Tubby looked up at Betty, and then transferred his gaze to Fatty. Porky looked at Fatty, and then at Tubby. Fatty looked down at his shoes.

"Horse?" said Tubby. "Fatty bought a horse?"

"Yes," said Betty. "It's a mighty strange story. Fatty bought a horse at the horse sale. I thought that was what you were talking about."

Tubby took a sip of his beer. "So," he said, a clear note of triumph in his voice. "There was a horse. You said …"

"I said nothing of the kind," Fatty suddenly exploded. "You asked me whether I had gone to the horse sale to buy a horse. I said, if you remember right, that I had gone to the horse sale because Lord Balnerry had invited us to go with him. Isn't that right, Betty?"

"Betty wasn't in the room," Tubby said quickly. "She can't say anything about what was said when she was out of the room. Remember President Nixon?"

"What about President Nixon?" snapped Fatty. "What's he got to do with it?"

Tubby snorted. "He said that he couldn't say what was said when he was out of the room. Remember? Same applies to Betty."

"That's not what I meant," retorted Fatty. "I said that

Betty will confirm that we went to the sales because we were invited by Lord Balnerry. We were his company, that's all. I said – and I'm obviously going to have to repeat it for the benefit of the hard of hearing – that I did not go to the sales to buy a horse. At no point did I say that I didn't end up buying a horse. That's all."

Tubby appeared dissatisfied. "You implied that you hadn't bought a horse. You said something about not being interested in horses."

"I'm not," said Fatty, a note of exasperation in his voice. "I'm just not interested in horses. Period."

"Then why did you go to the sales to buy a horse?" asked Tubby.

"I didn't go to buy a horse," said Fatty.

"But you did buy one, didn't you? There was a horse, wasn't there? Isn't that what Betty's just said?"

"Of course there were horses at a horse sale," Fatty said. "What do you expect? Chickens?"

Betty, who was standing above her guests, listening to the exchange, now sat down.

"Fatty's horse was a mistake," she said quietly. "It was very embarrassing for us. In fact, I think we should talk about something different."

She looked sharply at Tubby as she spoke, and their

guest dropped his eyes.

"I'm sorry," he said. "I didn't mean to criticise you, Fatty. Anybody could buy a horse by mistake."

"Yes," said Porky, who was also eager to bring the unfortunate argument to an end. "I heard of one guy who waved at the wrong moment at a car auction and bought a 1962 Cadillac. Cost him quite a bit."

"Waved?" asked Tubby. "Pretty stupid thing to do at an auction!"

Fatty reached for a sandwich, avoiding Betty's eye.

Tubby laughed. "Imagine going to an auction and waving and then finding you'd bought something! Who could be so stupid?"

The following day, Fatty went to see his physician. He was still experiencing a degree of discomfort from the cracked rib, although it felt markedly better since his return. Betty, however, thought it would be wise to have it checked: the doctor who had seen him in Ireland, charming though he was, might not have known what he was doing. Fatty assured her that her doubts were surely misplaced, but agreed nonetheless to make an appointment to see Dr Eustace Lafouche at his office near the university.

Dr Lafouche had an interest in antiques and the two usually chatted about his latest acquisitions after the consultation was over. On this occasion, after Dr Lafouche had said that the rib was nothing to worry about, they talked for a short time about a cabinet that the doctor had bought at a recent house sale in Little Rock. Fatty looked at the photograph that Dr Lafouche had of the piece, and agreed the attribution that the doctor suggested. This pleased Dr Lafouche, who grinned with pleasure. Then, after a moment, his expression changed.

"There's one other thing, Mr O'Leary," said Dr Lafouche. "I've been meaning to talk to you about it for some time."

Fatty smiled. "You've got another piece? Dubious provenance?"

Dr Lafouche shook his head. "No. Nothing like that," he said. "It's your health, actually. I'm a bit worried about your weight. I think we really should do something about it."

Fatty sagged in his chair.

"Oh," he said. Then, after a pause: "Oh that."

"Yes," said Dr Lafouche, looking at a record sheet in front of him. "Your weight has been going up and up. This trip to Ireland probably didn't help much. One always puts on weight on holiday. But you really should tackle it for the sake of your heart."

"I see," said Fatty. "You know, I don't feel overweight. I know I might look a bit on the stout side, but I feel quite good, you know."

Dr Lafouche sighed. "You may feel all right, but think about all the extra work your poor heart is doing. Thump, thump – all that weight to carry around. Thump, thump. Hearts are only human, you know. They feel it too."

Fatty was silent. He looked at the doctor mutely. When would the dreaded word "diet" be uttered? Doctors always put you on a diet sooner or later, even an unfussy doctor like Lafouche, who liked to drink and buy antiques. Sooner or later their training got to them and they remembered that they were supposed to put everybody on a diet.

"I think the only way for you to tackle this is to go on a course," said Dr Lafouche. "There's a place not far out of town which has recently opened up. It's run by a Dr Herb Meyer, a highly-qualified gastro-intestinal-colonic-hepaticologist. He's very good, I believe. The clinic is residential. Nice grounds. You spend a week or two there and they turn things round. They …"

"You mean they starve you," Fatty interjected.

Dr Lafouche laughed. "There's no need to starve," he countered. "All they do is change the way you think about food. They train you to eat more healthily. In fact, you'll probably find some of their menus pretty tasty. Those people can do things with lettuce …"

"I don't know," said Fatty. "I've just been away, and now to go away again."

"It's for your own good," said Dr Lafouche. "It's better going to the clinic than going off to hospital for weeks and weeks."

"It's a fat farm," said Fatty, miserably. "That's what it is. You want to send me to a fat farm."

"Well," said Dr Lafouche, "that's not a term I'd use. But they do a good job, whatever you call them."

"Are you really insisting that I go?" asked Fatty quietly. "Doctor's orders?"

Dr Lafouche pursed his lips. "I'm afraid so," he said. "I really must recommend it most strongly. Why not give it a try? See if it helps."

Fatty sat in silence. He had read in the paper about this new clinic, but had turned the page over quickly, in the way in which one does when confronted with pictures of train disasters or other scenes of human suffering. Now his ostrich-like attitude was catching up on him, and he was to enter the clinic portals himself. *Oh!* he thought, and then *Oh!* again.

12

BETTY DROVE A PENSIVE FATTY to the Meyer Clinic. It was a pleasant day and the Ozarks were at their best: a limestone landscape of short distances and quiet valleys, but Fatty seemed impervious to the charms of his surroundings. He felt as one might feel on the way to root-canal treatment at the hands of a dentist whose supplies of dental anaesthetic had run out. He did not even recall giving final and unambiguous consent to the undertaking. Dr Lafouche had telephoned and booked him in there and then, taking Fatty's silence as an indication of his willingness to undergo the treatment. And then it was too late: once the booking had been made, Fatty was committed. His American Express Card number had been taken and to the not inconsiderable expense of the purchase of the horse had been added the outrageous cost of two weeks in the Meyer Clinic (immediately debited and completely non-refundable). This was nine thousand dollars, which would not include extras. No mention was made of bar bills, presumably, Fatty reflected, because there would be nothing to drink.

The clinic had sent him what they described as a "welcome pack", which Fatty had browsed with a growing sense of doom. On the front page there was a picture of Dr Herb Meyer himself, a man in his early sixties with dark hair neatly parted down the middle and the eyes of a fanatic – or so Fatty thought. Here was a man who had clearly never enjoyed the pleasure of a generous T-bone steak, nor ploughed his way through a delicious plate of *tagliatelle*, liberally doused in melted butter and topped with genuine *Parmigiano Reggiano*. Here was a face which had never known the olfactory pleasures of a sizzling barbecue, accompanied by the tactile delights of a chilled can of high-calorie beer in one's hand. None of this in such a life! Instead, a life of lettuce and light salad dressing! Poor man, thought Fatty, for a moment even feeling a rush of sympathy for Dr Meyer.

After the picture of Dr Meyer, there followed photographs of the clinic's various rooms. Here was the games room in which two patients appeared to be playing a lacklustre game of table tennis. They held their bats weakly, as one might after a few days of Dr Meyer's regime, and Fatty noted the spare folds of skin about their necks, once filled, no doubt, by life-sustaining adipose deposits but now empty and quite *de trop*. Then there were pictures of the colonic irrigation room, with its threatening hoses and sluices, the counselling room – very similar to the front room of a funeral parlour – complete with boxes of tissues to deal with the distress of being in the clinic, and finally a picture of the entire staff lined up in serried ranks behind Dr Meyer, each one of them clad in white jackets of the sort popularly supposed to be worn by the attendants in psychiatric institutions.

"Oh Betty," groaned Fatty. "Why do I have to go to this place? What have I done to deserve this?"

"Eaten too much," replied Betty, cheerfully.

Fatty was shocked by her levity, but the idea for a clever remark came to him and he quickly passed over his sense of betrayal.

"*Et tu* Betty!" he said, pausing for her reaction to his erudite reference.

Betty looked blank. "Ate what too?"

"No, not ate, or eat, but *et*. The Latin word for *and*. I learned it at Notre Dame. And *tu* means *you*. You too! This is what Caesar said when he saw that his friend, Brutus, was one of the conspirators who stabbed him. He said, *Et tu, Brute!* That's what he said."

"But what's that got to do with eating?" asked Betty. She thought that she understood Fatty – and generally she did – but on occasion he seemed to drift off into irrelevancies.

Now, slumped in the passenger seat of their car, while

Betty drove calmly along the quiet rural back road, Fatty moved from anxiety to resignation. If this had to happen, then he would let it happen. He would simply think about being elsewhere and imagine himself doing something else, the tactic he had adopted during his humiliating experience in the bath in Ireland. So, while Dr Meyer tormented him with whatever indignities he was preparing for him, he would simply think about great meals he had had in the past. He would imagine the lettuce leaves to be slivers of wafer-thin Parma ham; he would close his eyes and imagine the carrots to be spears of asparagus dipped in butter. And anything they sought to do to him with hoses, or any saunas in which they caged him, would be but the imaginary buffeting of the elements on a restaurant-hike through France, one of those extraordinary organised tours which Fatty had read about in which the hikers made their way from restaurant to restaurant through the Normandy countryside. With this attitude, nothing could harm him, and he smiled as he reflected on the new armour in which he had clad himself.

"Thinking of something funny?" asked Betty.

"No," said Fatty, still smiling. "Just thinking of how the last laugh is going to be on me. These people may think they're going to wear me down, but the O'Learys are made of sterner stuff than that."

"That's the spirit, Fatty," said Betty. "That's the spirit that's made this country what it is."

But when a sign for the clinic appeared at the side of the road, Fatty's brief elevation of mood was rapidly deflated and he shrank visibly back in his seat. Betty, noticing this, took one hand off the wheel and patted him gently on the knee.

"Don't worry, Fatty," she said. "It's only two weeks, and then, when you come back, we can go out and have a lovely celebration dinner somewhere."

In the clinic, abandoned by Betty, Fatty was shown to his room. He was pleasantly surprised by its comfort and by the view it afforded of the grounds, with their trees and lawns. In addition to the bed and wardrobe, there was a writing desk, an easy chair and a small exercise bicycle. On the walls there were pictures designed to offend no tastes: a van Gogh hayfield, a picture of two lovers strolling arm in arm along what looked like the banks of the Seine and an old state map.

Fatty had just finished unpacking his suitcase when there came a knock on the door and he found himself facing a nurse, a chart tucked under her arm.

"Mr O'Leary," she said, "I have come to weigh you in. Do you mind?"

She pointed to the set of scales next to the exercise bicycle. Fatty took a deep breath and nodded. Then, in his stockinged feet, he stepped gingerly onto the scales. He did not cast his eye downwards, but looked up instead at the ceiling whence his help might come, but there was none – only the sharp intake of breath of the nurse as she read the figures and noted them on her chart.

"Well, Mr O'Leary," she said. "You can step off the scales now."

They moved back into the bedroom, where the nurse extracted a large pair of callipers from a bag. Then, having asked Fatty to pull up his shirt to reveal his midriff, she opened the jaws of the callipers and pinched his flesh. Fatty winced, and closed his eyes; he had been in the clinic no more than fifteen minutes and the indignities had begun. So might the souls in Purgatory be inducted into their regime: their suffering so much less than those consigned to Hell – callipers, perhaps, rather than heated tongs, but suffering none the less.

Her survey of Fatty completed, the nurse now invited him to accompany her to meet Dr Meyer, who would take a full medical history and who would prescribe his treatment over the next two weeks. Meekly, Fatty followed her down the sterile corridor to the door ominously marked with the Meyer name.

"Just knock," said the nurse. "Dr Meyer is expecting you."

Fatty raised a trembling hand to the door and prepared to knock, but at that precise moment the door was opened from within and he found himself confronted by the man whose photograph he had seen on the Clinic's pamphlet: Dr Herbert H. Meyer, M.D., Ph.D.

"Mr O'Leary?" said the doctor, stepping aside to allow Fatty to enter the room. "It is a great pleasure to meet you, sir."

Fatty shook hands with the doctor, feeling his thin, cold hand in his and catching for a moment the scent of cloves.

Dr Meyer gestured to a chair and invited Fatty to sit down.

"You walked directly from your room?" Dr Meyer asked. "From Wing B?"

Fatty nodded. "With the nurse," he said. "She told me you were expecting me."

Over the next fifteen minutes, Dr Meyer took Fatty's medical history and quizzed him about his eating habits. The latter involved searching questions and, on occasion, direct challenges to the veracity of Fatty's estimates.

"Only one helping of dessert, Mr O'Leary? Are you sure of that?"

The tone was that of a skilled interrogator or a persistent prosecutor breaking down the defendant's story.

"And cake? Mr O'Leary? What about cake? Up to seven hundred calories per slice?"

At the end, Fatty, sweating with anxiety, noticed that his hands were shaking. Dr Meyer was watching him closely and suddenly announced that he would have to leave the room for a few minutes to check on one of the other patients.

"Nurse Maggio will come in," he said. "She will look after you while I'm out of the room. She will offer you a herbal tea."

He pressed a button on his desk and after a few moments the nurse who had accompanied Fatty from his room came through the door. Fatty accepted her offer of herbal tea, and while she prepared the infusion she talked to him in a gentle, friendly fashion.

"Dr Meyer's been asking you about food?" she said. "That's what he usually does."

Fatty nodded. "Searching questions," he said. "Fairly intimidating."

"Dear, dear," said Nurse Maggio. "I wish that he would be more gentle with the patients."

Fatty smiled. "It's his job, I suppose," he said.

Nurse Maggio handed him the mug of camomile tea.

"And cake?" she said casually. "Did he mention cake?"

"Yes," said Fatty ruefully. "He mentioned cake."

The nurse laughed. "And I suppose you told him that you always only had one slice rather than two? And you said that you had never heard of Betty Crocker?"

"Yes," said Fatty. "I suppose that I rather misled him on the cake. I said ... "

He stopped. The awful realisation, vivid and overwhelming in its implications, had just dawned on him. He had fallen for the oldest trick in the interrogator's book: the nice cop, nasty cop routine. The hard questions come from the nasty cop who is then replaced for a while by the nice cop. The suspect, relieved at the sympathetic tone of the nice cop's remarks, lets slip the truth, just as he had now done. Now it was too late! He had told the nurse the truth, and that would get right back to Dr Meyer.

"I see," said the nurse. "Two slices? And chocolate? Did he ask you about chocolate?"

Fatty said nothing, but took a sip of his camomile tea. He did not have to reply. He could keep silent, as the constitution allowed him. Or, he could turn the tables on his interrogators and ask them about themselves.

"Let's stop talking about me," he said at last. "Tell me about yourself, Nurse Maggio. Do you like chocolate?"

The nurse stiffened.

"Chocolate?" she said, her voice strained. "Why would you think I should like chocolate?"

Fatty narrowed his eyes with cunning. It was clear that his question had wrong-footed her.

"Because most people do," he said. "If they're honest, they'll admit to liking chocolate."

"Not here," said Nurse Maggio. "We don't encourage chocolate in the clinic. For obvious reasons."

"Oh I can understand that," said Fatty. "But what about at home? Do you not eat chocolate at home?"

The nurse now began to look flustered. She turned her head and looked at the door.

"I might eat chocolate to some extent," she said. "Not being an overweight person, I am able to indulge a taste for chocolate now and then. You can't."

Fatty bristled with indignation. Who was she to tell him what he could or could not do?

"Why not?" he said loudly. "Why should I not be able to enjoy myself like anybody else? Why should I be made to suffer?"

"Because of your weight," said Nurse Maggio primly. "I'm sorry to have to say this, Mr O'Leary, but it's because you're greedy. You've just admitted to me that you like to have more than one slice of cake. You said so yourself. I heard you."

"Ah!" said Fatty. "So you weren't just making conversation, were you? You're working for him through there, aren't you?"

Nurse Maggio laughed. "Of course I'm working for him. That's my job."

"Disgusting," said Fatty. "You try to trick your patients into admitting to things and then you run right back to him, to that miserable calorie counter, and tell him his patient's secrets."

Nurse Maggio's jaw dropped. "You mustn't call him that," she hissed. "You are a very rude man, Mr O'Leary. And, what's more, I could tell you something about yourself. Oh, I could tell you."

"You tell me something about myself?" said Fatty angrily. "You? You've known me for twenty minutes at the most, and you think that you can tell me something about myself. Well, let's hear it then. Come on!"

Nurse Maggio pointed a finger at Fatty.

"All right," she said. "Since you ask, I'll tell you. You know what? *I don't think that you really want to become thin.*"

The bombshell released, she sat back in her chair and waited for its effect.

Fatty said nothing for a moment. Then, leaning forward, he placed the mug containing the rest of his herbal tea on the desk and rose to his feet. As he did so, Dr Meyer silently re-entered the room. Nurse Maggio saw him come in, but Fatty, who was facing the other way, did not.

"You're right!" said Fatty, his voice raised in defiance. "I have no wish to become thin. I am a fat man; that's what I am. I am proud of what I am, and unlike so many people these days, I have no intention of trying to be something I am not. God, Nurse Maggio, made fat men and he made thin. He also made some in-between. I am a fat man. I am a happy fat man who enjoys the pleasures of the table. I enjoy the smell of steak, and I enjoy eating it. I love large portions of apple pie with whipped cream. I love pistachio nuts. I enjoy red wine. I could go on: there are many other sorts of food. I am happy. This is my nature, and I am not – I shall not be – ashamed of it. And I shall not allow any calorie-obsessed doctor and his sidekick to make me feel unhappy. I shall not! Not now! Not ever!"

No Roman orator could have spoken with greater dignity, but Cato himself would never have felt such conviction as did Fatty. For a moment, there was a silence such as that which must have followed the address at Gettysburg. But even if Nurse Maggio was, in spite of herself, impressed, this was not so with Dr Meyer, who took the silence as his signal to reveal his presence. He had been standing quite still, but now stepped forward to refute the heresies to which he had been obliged to listen.

"So!" he said, his reedy nasal voice raised, but nowhere near the strength of Fatty's stentorian tones. "So, you do not want to become thin! And not only that, but you laugh at those of us who are the correct weight. You even manifest your defiance with insults, which, needless to say, I treat with complete contempt. You stand there and say these things in this very office where I have helped so many people like you. You stand there and roar defiance. How dare you, Mr O'Leary? How dare you?"

Fatty glanced at Nurse Maggio, who was smirking with relief at the arrival of reinforcements. She was a mere foot soldier; Dr Meyer was the heavy artillery in the ranks of the thin.

"Hah," said Fatty. "You want me to admit to eating too much. Very well, I do, and I say to you: so what? Now, what about you? Why don't you admit to being hungry? Go on. You certainly look it. Why don't you admit to loving the idea of a slice of cake? Wouldn't you feel satisfied if you ate something like that? Wouldn't it give you pleasure, just as Nurse Maggio here said that she found pleasure in chocolate?"

Nurse Maggio gasped. "I would never say that, Dr Meyer! He's twisting my words. I never said anything like that."

"You said it," said Fatty. "And I heard it. And if Dr Meyer were honest, he would say the same thing himself. But he won't. Oh no, we won't get the truth from a person like him."

Dr Meyer suddenly clapped his hands together sharply.

"Mr O'Leary, you have gone far enough. I would be prepared to take a tolerant view and allow you to remain, but I must bear in mind the morale of the other patients. I cannot allow a man like you to undermine our efforts here. You will please leave."

"With pleasure," said Fatty. "Once you have refunded my seven thousand dollars."

Dr Meyer ignored him for a moment, walking briskly round the room to his desk, where he took up his position in his chair.

"Impossible," he said. "The terms of the clinic are very clearly stated in the agreement which you signed on your admission. In the event of misconduct requiring a patient to be discharged, nothing is refundable. I'm very sorry."

Fatty now spoke very quietly, but his words were clearly articulated. "In that case," he said. "I shall stay and I shall inform the other patients of our little exchange. I shall inform them, over lunch, or over lettuce, that Nurse Maggio here admitted to me that she likes chocolate. I shall inform them of your real opinion of stout people. I shall urge them to stand up and fight back. I shall urge them not to accept the reign of terror of the thin. I shall urge them to be themselves and not to worry about it. In short, sir, I shall undermine you! And then ..."

When this unfinished threat was made, Nurse Maggio gave a start, and took a few steps to place herself more firmly in the shelter of her employer. For his part, barely flinching, Dr Meyer stared at Fatty through narrowed eyes.

"You are a very dangerous man, Mr O'Leary," he said. "You are highly calorific."

"Yes," said Fatty. "I am. Now please will you give me my refund?"

Dr Meyer stared for a moment at his hands. Then he opened a drawer in his desk and took out a chequebook.

He scribbled a few words and figures and then handed the cheque over the table to Fatty. Fatty glanced at it, nodded, and put it away in his shirt pocket.

"Goodbye," said Fatty, rising to leave. " I wish you a pleasant day. I myself shall go out for lunch when I get back to Fayetteville. Then, this evening, I shall go out for dinner with my wife, Betty. We shall have a very good time."

"You'll regret this," said Dr Meyer. "You'll have an ischaemic event one of these days. You will probably die, you know."

"We will all die, you spiteful man," said Fatty. "Sorry to have to be the bearer of bad news, but we are all going to die. You. Me. Nurse Maggio over here. All of us."

He turned round and left the office, nodding to Nurse Maggio as he passed her.

"Not too much chocolate!" he said, wagging his finger at her.

Outside, while he waited for his cab to arrive, he felt the warm sun on his face and he breathed in deeply. Several other patients were sitting on a bench outside the front door, taking the air.

"You just arrived?" asked one.

"Just arrived, and just leaving," said Fatty. "Going back

to Fayetteville to have a big lunch."

"Oh!" said one of the patients, a large woman in a loud, floral dress. "You lucky man!"

Fatty chuckled. "Why don't you folks come too?" he said. "There'll be plenty of room in the cab."

The three on the bench looked at one another. Then one of them nodded, and the others rose to their feet.

"Well done," said Fatty. "Italian? Mexican? French? Where shall we go?"

"Italian," said the woman in the floral dress. "I've been dreaming about pasta ever since I came."

"Then Italian it will be," said Fatty.

13

Two WEEKS AFTER HIS SUCCESSFUL escape from the Meyer Clinic, Fatty received a letter from Lord Balnerry, enclosing a dollar draft for the equivalent of fifteen thousand Irish pounds. In the letter, Lord Balnerry explained that he had sold their horse on, at a considerable profit, to a trainer in Kerry. This was Fatty's share of the profit, added to the seven thousand pounds that he owed him from the original purchase.

"I so enjoyed meeting you and Betty," wrote Lord Balnerry. "We all had such a good time together. So don't wait too long before you come back over to Ireland. My door is always open. Remember that."

Fatty and Betty reflected on their good fortune. It was not just the money, of course; it was the warmth of the invitation. Ireland seemed rosy now, and perhaps they would go back, not just now, of course, but in a year or two. Even Rupert O'Brien held no terrors for Fatty now; he would be able to deal with him, even without any help from Lord Balnerry.

Fatty thought about his good fortune. He had a loyal and supportive wife, a woman who loved him, in spite of everything. To Betty he was simply the most important person in the world; he knew that, as he had known it from the very beginning of their courtship and their marriage. And to him, she was his world; his inspiration, his companion, his reason for living. And he had good friends too: Tubby and Porky, for all their little differences of opinion, would give him the shirt off their back, their last cent, if he ever needed either. And he would do the same for them.

"I have had a fortunate life," he said to Betty. "Don't you think so, Betty?"

"Oh I do," said Betty. "I do indeed."

Fatty and Betty sat on their porch, the morning sun on their faces, looking down the leafy street, with its comfortable well-kept homes. Somebody had been cutting a lawn, and there was the sweet smell of mown grass on the air. Fatty sniffed it appreciatively. A dog barked. Porky Flanagan drove past in his old Chrysler, slowed down, and waved. Fatty waved back. Then he closed his eyes, and smiled.